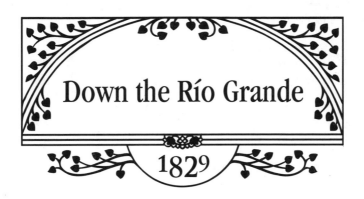

Down the Río Grande

1829

Books by Laurie Lawlor

The Worm Club
How to Survive Third Grade
Addie Across the Prairie
Addie's Long Summer
Addie's Dakota Winter
George on His Own
Gold in the Hills
Little Women *(a movie novelization)*

Heartland series
Heartland: Come Away with Me
Heartland: Take to the Sky
Heartland: Luck Follows Me

American Sisters series
West Along the Wagon Road 1852
A *Titanic* Journey Across the Sea 1912
Voyage to a Free Land 1630
Adventure on the Wilderness Road 1775
Crossing the Colorado Rockies 1864
Down the Río Grande 1829

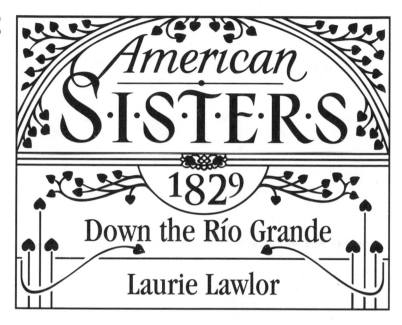

American
S·I·S·T·E·R·S
1829
Down the Río Grande

Laurie Lawlor

A MINSTREL® HARDCOVER
PUBLISHED BY POCKET BOOKS

New York   London   Toronto   Sydney   Singapore

A MINSTREL HARDCOVER

A Minstrel Book published by
POCKET BOOKS, a division of Simon & Schuster, Inc.
1230 Avenue of the Americas, New York, NY 10020

Copyright © 2000 by Laurie Lawlor

ISBN: 0-671-03922-9

First Minstrel Books hardcover printing September 2000

10 9 8 7 6 5 4 3 2 1

A MINSTREL BOOK and colophon are registered trademarks
of Simon & Schuster, Inc.

Cover illustration by Frank Sofo

Printed in the U.S.A.

For Boone

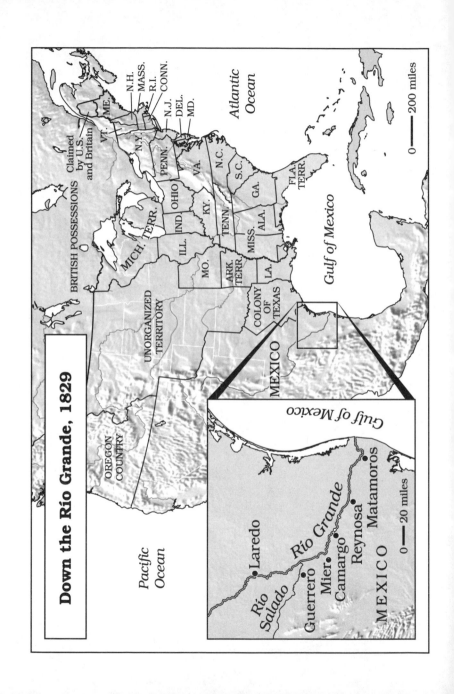

Down the Río Grande, 1829

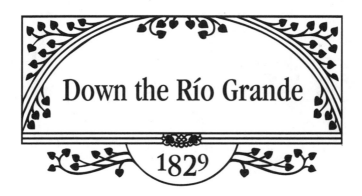

Down the Río Grande

1829

Introduction

The Río Grande is a river with many names. In its
long, colorful history it has been called *P'osog* or
"big river" by the Tewa Indians; Grand River and
River of May by English explorers and Río Bravo,
Río Bravo del Norte, Río Caudaloso or "carrying
much water," Río de Nuestra Señora, Río de San
Buenaventura del Norte and Río del Norte by the
Spanish and Mexicans who settled along its ever-
changing banks.

From its headwaters high in the Colorado
Rockies to the Gulf of Mexico, the Río Grande
flows 1,896 miles through some of the most hostile,
arid land in southwestern North America. The
river has been the source of life for many people for
countless generations.

Down the Río Grande, 1829 is the little-told story of the great river before it became a dividing line between the United States and Mexico. In 1829, when this story takes place, Mexico had just freed itself from rule by Spain. Every small outpost and village along the lower Río Grande was part of Mexico. The colony of Texas—made up of about three hundred American families—was officially less than six years old and still belonged to Mexico.

In 1836 Texas declared itself a separate country called the Republic of Texas. A few years later, in 1845, Congress decided to "annex" Texas as the twenty-eighth state. Not until 1848, after a bitter war between Mexico and the United States, would the Río Grande be designated the official boundary between the two countries. Texas statehood would have far-reaching effects on the course of American history. By allowing Texas to enter the Union with slavery as a legal reality, the United States was given one of the final pushes toward the Civil War.

Down the Río Grande, 1829 is based on the true story of the *Ariel,* one of the very first steamboats to be used in Texas waters. It was the property of Henry Austin, who, like so many others, came to Texas in the summer of 1829 to seek his fortune.

Chapter 1

On a dusty street of the little village of Guerrero a
stray dog howled and barked and howled some
more. "What's the matter with that dog?" María
asked and cocked her head to one side. She stood
near the open window of the bedroom she had
shared for the past three years in a kind of uneasy
peace with her sister, Frida, and Rosita, their new
stepsister.

"This white dress does not suit me," Rosita said.
She sat in front of the mirror and brushed her long,
dark hair. Carefully, she licked the tip of one finger
and ran it over her perfectly arched eyebrows. Life
seemed so unfair. She was only sixteen and was
being forced by her father to marry an old man
with bristles growing from his ears. All her happi-

ness would soon end forever. Why couldn't Papa understand? Didn't he love her anymore?

"The poor thing sounds as if its lungs will burst." María leaned her elbows on the windowsill and took a deep breath. From the kitchen came the aroma of roasted lamb, grilled duck, and fried onions and chiles. Perhaps the smell of the wedding feast cooking made the hungry dog howl. "Do you think I should take the animal a tortilla or a bit of meat?"

Rosita kept brushing her hair and did not reply. María sighed. She felt as invisible and unwanted as the barking dog. She knew Rosita wasn't listening. She never listened.

"I should wear black like the old women at the burials," Rosita said. She fingered the soft red fringe on the yellow silk shawl embroidered with bright green and blue birds. At her neck hung the agate necklace that had belonged to her mother, who died four years earlier. The glittering brown-flecked stones were nearly the color of her beloved mother's mysterious eyes. If her mother were still alive, everything would be different, Rosita decided. Her father would be happy and call her his *charamusca*, his sugar cake, the way he used to when she was little. She would have no spoiled, annoying stepsisters or spiteful stepmother who clearly despised her.

"Perhaps a stranger is coming," María said. She squinted into the distance and wondered how long a dog could bark a warning before its voice gave out altogether. She was fifteen, mousey, and a bit stoop-shouldered. Her habit of squinting gave her face a pensive scowl that her mother blamed on too much reading. "I curse the day your grandfather taught you to read," her mother always told her. "You'll never find a husband. Men do not like women who spend all their time staring at books."

Suddenly the door swung open. Seventeen-year-old Frida staggered inside and lowered herself on to the bed. She fanned her plump, flushed face with her best brocade fan and shot a critical glance at Rosita. As usual, Rosita did not seem the least impressed by her eldest stepsister's dramatic entrance. This lack of respect only made proud Frida more furious.

"What's wrong?" María demanded in a concerned voice. She sat patiently beside Frida and waited for her to catch her breath.

"A monster on the river. They say it cuts through rocks and breathes fire," Frida said, then paused. She folded the fan and added in a hushed tone, "And there are four *norteamericanos*. They are coming this way."

María gasped and jumped up. Quickly, she shuttered the window and made the sign of the cross to keep away any evil.

"And the wedding?" Rosita asked, not once taking her gaze from the mirror.

"*Mañana* or perhaps the day after," Frida replied. Her eyes narrowed to jealous slits. "I hope you're not as disappointed as don Cassos. He's gone to bed from the shock of the news that the wedding must be postponed. Poor, dear man."

For the first time Rosita smiled at her radiant reflection. *I am saved.*

Captain Henry Austin gave the dog that followed them a good, hard kick. A whole mob of mangy curs circled and snarled around him and his three companions. "Where are we?" Albert Oliver demanded. He was wheezing hard and his feet hurt. "This does not look promising. Not in the least. I thought you said we'd find customers. I don't see anyone. May I remind you that the river water level is dropping? We have no time to waste."

"For a ship's clerk, you have little faith," Captain Austin said cheerfully.

"For a captain, you have too much," Oliver grumbled.

"Where is the cantina? I want a drink." Alpheus Rackliffe, the ship's boastful young pilot, weaved dangerously in and out of the mesquite. His bright red hair stuck out from under his foppish cap, which he had pushed back on his head. Already his forehead and nose were turning dangerously pink.

"Pretty considerable jugful of sun this morning, isn't there?" boomed McCallister, a stolid man in a large-brimmed hat. "And if we don't find another couple of deckhands, we're going to be in big trouble, Captain. We've already lost four and I can't carry the cargo like a roustabout *and* run the capstan *and* help man the pumps *and* stoke the furnace—"

"Shut up," snapped Rackliffe. "You make my head hurt. While we're looking for deckhands perhaps we can also find a new mate who isn't a Texan and doesn't talk so wicked much."

McCallister's cold, reptilian eyes narrowed and his face became dark and menacing. He clenched his fists but he did not do anything, even though he wanted to rearrange Rackliffe's slender sunburned nose. He knew he couldn't. Rackliffe was the pilot, a right smart man who was paid more than the rest of them. He was the only one who claimed to know how to steer the old rattrap out of this godforsaken place.

"Now, gentlemen," Captain Austin announced good-naturedly, "you'll let me handle the natives, won't you? I know what to do."

Oliver mumbled something in such a low voice that nobody could hear him. Reluctantly, he waddled behind the others as they made their way into the empty plaza. The grim, treeless square was located in the middle of the village of white, flat-roofed houses and small huts. A fancy stone church anchored one end of the plaza. The tall, grandiose building looked lonely and out of place in such simple, rustic surroundings.

"Hello? Anybody here?" Captain Austin shouted in Spanish. At the sound of his voice, the dogs that had been following them rolled in the dust and scratched their fleas and loped into the shadows.

Slowly the enormous wooden door of the church of Nuestra Señora del Refugio opened a crack. A Mexican in a sombrero came out. He rearranged his serape, the colorful piece of cloth he wore slung over his shoulder. Captain Austin nudged Oliver, who wiped the back of his sweaty neck with a dirty handkerchief. But instead of coming toward them or even acknowledging their presence, the man in the sombrero slunk away. "*¡Hola!*" Captain Austin shouted after him, but the man neither stopped nor glanced back. Captain Austin sighed. "I suppose we shall just have to knock. Perhaps there are others inside the church who may be of assistance to us."

"It ain't Sunday, is it?" McCallister grumbled.

"What if the cantina is closed? We came all this way—" Rackliffe stopped speaking. His jaw dropped as the church door opened. Out into the plaza stepped what had to be every man and boy in the village of Guerrero. They had fierce expressions and they were carrying pikes and pitchforks and machetes with gleaming blades. A few cradled ancient muskets in their arms.

Captain Austin gulped. He quickly unhitched the buckle to his pistol holster and held this gun high in the air so that the villagers could see it. He motioned for Rackliffe, Oliver, and McCallister to lay down their weapons as well. Reluctantly, they did as they were told. "I don't like this," Oliver whispered, holding his pale, damp hands in the air. "Not a bit."

"Don't worry. Smile. Keep smiling," Captain Austin said between gritted teeth. "They're just a bit nervous, that's all."

"Yeah, maybe they thought we was more Spanish invaders or Comanches or somebody pretty considerable." McCallister sneered. He held up his rifle but he did not remove the knife he always kept hidden inside his boot. As ship's mate he was accustomed to using his big, meaty hands and anything else he could find that was large and hard to bash into the skulls of the stupid deckhands he had to corral into doing an honest day's work.

The leader of Guerrero stepped forward. He was a distinguished older man with a white moustache who introduced himself as the *alcade*, don Octavio García, the mayor. "You are *gringos*. Where are you from, strangers?"

Captain Austin gave his most convincing grin and made a gracious, short bow. He cleared his throat and spoke in fluent Spanish. Every so often he was prompted by Oliver, who also spoke the language. "*Buenos días*, fellow Mexicans. We are from the colony of Texas."

The crowd mumbled in a menacing way. For the past five years *gringos* had become more and more frequently seen passing through small villages like Guerrero. Their numbers began to climb in 1824, when Mexico officially invited Americans to settle in Texas, which was considered a wild, northern wasteland dominated by hostile Comanche.

"Who are you?" don García demanded.

"I am Captain Henry Austin. Perhaps you have heard of my cousin, Stephen Austin of Texas? A remarkable man."

Don García frowned. He had heard much of ambitious Austin, the leader of the ever-growing Texas colony. "What do you want? Why are you here?"

"I am the captain of the steamboat *Ariel*. We're plying the waters of the Río Grande. I have come seeking supplies and a few deckhands. I am also looking for cargo, passengers, and mail. Anything that needs to go up or down the river. Business, you might say."

The crowd behind don García murmured. Their voices sounded confused and indignant. "*Yanquis. Yanquis,*" they kept saying over and over again.

"The Río Grande?" don García said suspiciously. "You mean the Río Bravo del Norte?"

"In Texas we call it the Río Grande. You may call it what you like," Captain Austin said generously. "What I'm suggesting is doing a little business with you folks . . ."

Another Mexican man stepped forward. He was middle-aged and his dark eyes were quick and perceptive. "Did you come up the river with a monster?" don José Treviño demanded.

The crowd murmured again.

Oliver chuckled. McCallister nudged him hard with his elbow.

"It is a steamboat, sir," Captain Austin explained with a perfectly straight face. "Carries one hundred thousand pounds of freight. The most beautiful, fastest boat you've ever seen in your life. A floating palace. We've got room for cargo that needs to be shipped to Matamoros. We've got room for passengers. The *Ariel* can run no matter how shallow the river goes. Why, she's been known to even run on heavy dew."

Don Treviño did not smile.

Captain Austin coughed nervously. "The river will be tamed one day. This will be a wealthy town. People will come here to farm. They will send their goods far away. In America there is a great river called the Mississippi. Hundreds of steamboats go up and down the great Mississippi every day. The river has made many rich men. You, too, could be rich."

"Hundreds of boats? Is such a thing possible?" don Treviño asked, raising one curious eyebrow.

Don García waved a hand dismissively in the air. "The river will never be tamed. One day it eats our land, sweeps away our crops, our houses. The next season it dries up to nearly nothing. No, the Río Bravo will never be tamed."

Captain Austin cocked his head to one side with great confidence and said, "Why don't you come down to the river and see for yourself? You can come on board and we'll give you a little tour."

Don García spoke quickly to don Treviño. Then don García turned to Captain Austin. "We wish to send a few men along with you to see this thing you call a steamboat."

"Certainly, sir," Captain Austin said, brightening considerably. "Bring as many folks as you wish."

Oliver rolled his eyes. "The supplies. The deck-hands. The business. Don't forget," he hissed in English to Captain Austin.

"And while we visit your fair city, we'd like to purchase some food supplies," Captain Austin said. "Perhaps bacon. Perhaps beans. Whatever you have available. Molasses? Cornmeal?"

"And whiskey," Rackliffe said. "We want whiskey."

Don García smiled for the first time. "Certainly. After we see your boat. Do not worry, *señor*. There is always *mañana*."

"*Mañana, mañana*," Oliver grumbled. Then he turned to McCallister and said in English, "To the Mexicans that can mean tomorrow, or in two weeks, or in two months, or in two years, or never."

McCallister clamped him hard on the shoulder with his steel grip. He grinned stupidly and pointed. A gaggle of Guerrero girls had opened the door of the church. They whispered and giggled as they stared out at the strangers. McCallister put one finger to his hat and called out to them in English, "And how does your copperosity sagacite this fine August morning?"

The girls laughed. Two scowling men closed the door of the church. Several others with pitchforks stood guard as Captain Austin and his men led six of the oldest and most respected leaders of Guerrero back to the river.

Don Treviño, who was no fool, kept his daughters locked inside his house as long as the *norteamericanos* were in the village. He did not wish to take any chances that the deal that he had painstakingly worked out with wealthy don Cassos, Rosita's suitor, would be destroyed by some careless word, some careless glance. There were warnings in songs about strangers coming to town. About what happened when young girls disappeared with them and never returned. But would someone like Rosita listen to such warnings? No. She was as stubborn and troublesome as her mother.

Don Treviño looked at his present situation with clear eyes. He had three daughters now. He had to find them three proper husbands. And the simple fact was that in Guerrero there were too many women and too few men. After the battles with Spanish troops for Mexico's independence in 1827 and repeated attacks from raiding Indians, there simply weren't enough eligible young men left.

And what happened at the *fandango* last month hadn't helped. Why did Rosita have to refuse to dance with that boy, Hippólito? The fight that broke out between Hippólito and the rest of the young swains resulted in a stabbing. Luckily, no one was seriously hurt. But people in the village talked. They always talked. "Get that reckless daughter of yours married, don Treviño," people told him, "before she comes to more grief."

Don Treviño traveled all the way to Mier to find don Cassos, a rich hacienda owner with more than a hundred head of cattle, a big house, a dozen servants, and more than a square league of land. Rosita was too young to understand now, but certainly one day she would be grateful to him for seeing to her future.

"You stay here inside the house until the *norteamericanos* are gone," don Treviño ordered his daughter and two stepdaughters. "Soon they will be on their way to the ocean. Good riddance."

"Yes, Papa," Frida answered obediently. She took out her embroidery.

"Yes, Papa," María echoed. She began reading her favorite book of poetry.

"Do you hear me, Rosita?" don Treviño said. "You are not allowed to leave the house."

"Yes, Papa," Rosita said halfheartedly and began to pace the bedroom.

"Why not play your violin for us?" María suggested.

Rosita glanced at the old violin dear Tía Lupe had given her. But even the idea of playing gave her no pleasure. She felt trapped, suffocated. Everything reminded her of escape. The way the birds flew up from the acacia. The way the smoke rose from the cooking fire. The way music floated into the night. The disturbing news about the great steamboat made Rosita more restless than ever. That very afternoon she and her stepsisters began to hear stories from the servants about the *yanquis* and their amazing boat that was as big as the church and twice as beautiful, with so much gilt and splendor that mere mortals could hardly imagine.

Villagers who had seen the great steamboat said that Captain Austin had a sprinkling can on the front to show how easily the ship supplied its own water when the river went dry. Others claimed that the steamboat was specially built so that when the river dropped and the sandbars came out for air, one of the other *norteamericanos* simply tapped a keg of beer and ran the boat for a league on the suds.

Rosita listened to all these stories and kept very quiet. No matter what Papa warned, she wanted to see the spectacular steamboat with her own eyes. She had heard that the *yanquis* were looking for passengers and that they would be leaving soon.

Any day now. This might be her last chance to escape from don Cassos, from her hateful stepmother and irritating stepsisters, from the whispers of the people in the village, and from her father, who did not seem to understand or care for her anymore.

Chapter

2

The next afternoon the pale, cloudless August sky shimmered with heat. No one in Guerrero could remember a spring and summer with so little rain. Not one drop. Corn had shriveled. The constant east wind scoured across the plains of mesquite and cactus and sang laments among the rows of rattling bean plants struggling to survive along the banks of the shrinking Río Salado, a tributary of the brave, wild river they called Río Bravo.

Dust rose in blinding gusts from nearby low hills. The wind did not discriminate among the poor or the rich of Guerrero. Grit seeped through the open windows and coated the *frijoles* and tortillas, the refried beans and flat corn bread, of families who crowded into the simple huts thatched with willow branches and mud called *jacales*. Grit seeped under the stout oak doors with the iron grillwork of the stone houses and coated the young goat meat dinners of the well-to-do families. Every morning poor and rich alike awoke exhausted and sweaty with their faces powdered in strange patterns and their teeth gray. No one could escape the wind, the dirt, the heat.

As they did every day during the most oppressive, breathless hours of sunlight, the people of Guerrero were taking their siestas. They shuttered their windows with carved wooden panels hung from leather hinges. They closed their small shops. No vendor wandered among the streets calling, *"¡Arroz con leche! ¡Arroz con leche!"* No shouting, barefoot children chased one another in the plaza. All was silent. Even stray dogs crawled into whatever shade they could find. Everyone slept or rested.

Everyone except Rosita.

As silently as she could, she slipped out the door of her father's grand house with the snail carved over the stone portico. She wrapped her white cotton shawl over her head and bare arms. Carefully she gathered a bundle of her most precious belongings, stuffed them inside a woven *morrales*, and hurried away from her napping family, snoring don Cassos, and the servants who were leaning against a cool stone kitchen wall or were stretched out on a hard wooden bench. For once she felt free of the prying stares that seemed to follow her everywhere.

There was something different about Rosita. Anyone in Guerrero could see that. Her passing made very old men stop and stare and wish they were young. Very young men stopped and stared and wished they were old. When Rosita walked down the street, dogs looked up from the cool shadows of buildings. Shutters opened. Women raised their hands to their mouths and spoke to each other in lowered voices. In the little village there was no need of wind with so many whispers.

But this time, no one was awake. No one saw her. No one whispered. Without looking back she left the blinding white buildings and empty straight streets of the village. The farther from town she traveled, the happier she felt. By the time she headed east past the rocks and falls and reached the barren hills of Río Salado, the invisible burden she carried always on her shoulders seemed to lighten ever so slightly. She could almost breathe freely.

Steadily she walked—not too fast, not too slow. And whenever she could, she slipped into the shade of a scrubby cactus and waited for her heart to stop beating so hard, for her feet to cool. She held the *morrales* close against herself so that the bulky bag and the front of her dress were wet with perspiration. Even though she wore leather huaraches, she felt the burning ground sear up through the thick soles. Her nostrils filled with the herby sweetness of mesquite and the smokey smell of dried creosote and the rich, muddy breath of the river.

She paused to remove a sharp pebble from her sandal.

Just then something crackled. A footstep?

She froze, terrified someone might be following her. There were bandits along the river. And the Comanche were always on the lookout for unwary travelers. Along the road to Dolores, Papa told her of white crosses, the eyes of God he called them, that marked the places where the unfortunate had been robbed and killed.

Rosita took a deep breath. Turning slowly, she caught a glimpse of a brown shape slithering under a rock.

Rattlesnake.

She made a sign of the cross and kept moving, careful to keep her distance. Perhaps it was too hot even for an angry rattlesnake.

She hurried on, faster now. Nearby she smelled the strong rotten-egg odor of two sulphur springs where hot underground water boiled and bubbled. Her aunt, dear Tía Lupe, who knew so much about so many things, once told her of the power of these strange gurgling places to heal aching bones and broken hearts. *Ah, poor Tía Lupe! If only these springs had the power to bring you back.*

It was Tía Lupe who told her after her father had remarried how she should love her stepsisters. How she should cherish them. She spoke of Rosita's mother, her sister, with such tenderness. She called her her history. "We were partners in time. Fellow travelers. Witnesses," she said. But Rosita could never imagine being a fellow traveler with either Frida or María. She was glad to leave Guerrero and journey far away. She didn't care if she ever saw her stepsisters again.

Rosita walked on and on. In the distance she heard the current, the ebb and crash and ripple of moving water and saw the silver thread, the path the Río Bravo took. She hurried faster. She could smell the river—stronger now. The scent of exotic and faraway places the river had traveled. Somewhere far to the north, she had been told, were impossibly steep, snow-covered mountains that were the source of the Río Bravo. And many leagues to the south the river emptied into the ocean. Papa said the ocean was not like the river. It tasted salty and stretched so wide that sailors who were brave enough to travel far enough could look in all directions and see no land—just open water and glinting sunlight. What kind of freedom would that be?

Gathering the shawl around her head and shoulders to shield her from the sun's glare, she searched up and down the river. This bend was the place she had been told the steamboat was moored.

But she saw nothing.

Her shoulders sagged. She was too late. The boat was gone. The muddy current swirled and rippled. It crashed and gurgled and cascaded. Her mouth filled with the taste of bitterness. She hugged her bundle tight and listened to the river mock her.

"Rosita!"

Instantly Rosita crouched low on the ground beside a boulder. *María!* Always following her everywhere like a shadow. Ruining everything.

"Rosita?"

Rosita bit her lip to keep from shouting in anger at her annoying stepsister. *Go away!*

"Rosita, where are you?"

Now her stepsister's voice sounded frightened. Rosita smiled. *Serves you right.* She tried to make herself smaller. Perhaps if she remained perfectly still, timid María would give up and go home—back to her books. She wouldn't have to talk to María. She wouldn't have to explain what she was doing here.

The wind chanted and the river crashed and

rumbled past. Rosita strained her ears in hopes of hearing María's footsteps becoming fainter and fainter, moving away from her. But she heard nothing. Rosita scowled. *Did she fall in the water?* Rosita knew her ill-tempered stepmother would never forgive her. María could not swim. If she drowned, it would be Rosita's fault. That was what her stepmother would say. "You are cursed like all the women in your family."

Rosita hesitated. She listened for the sound of a cry, a splash. And when she could wait and listen no longer, she stood up and shouted, "María?"

"Yes?"

There was María, perched on a nearby rock, grinning like a fool. For once she carried no books. Her coarse black hair was tangled around her sweaty face. She had ripped her long skirt. And she wore nothing to protect her head. Perhaps the sun had made her *loca*.

"Why do you follow me like this?" Rosita demanded furiously. "Leave me alone."

"I thought you'd be glad to see me," María said. Her smile vanished. "What is that you're carrying?"

"Nothing," Rosita replied. She tucked the bundle behind her back. "Does your mother know where you are?"

María shook her head shyly. "I know how to be

silent, too. You thought I was sleeping, didn't you? Maybe you'd like some company. That's why I followed you."

"Company?" Rosita exploded. She tilted her head back and opened her mouth and laughed. Her loud donkey laughter echoed along the river. "Whatever made you think that?"

María looked at her dirty feet and shrugged. *I should not have come.*

When Rosita saw her stepsister's sad expression, she stopped laughing. "I am sorry. I didn't mean to insult you. Sometimes I just say things that get me into trouble." She coughed apologetically. "Are you all right? Maybe too much sun. Sit over here." Rosita pointed to a small patch of shade beside some mesquite. If María collapsed from sun sickness, how would she ever carry her back to the village? Luckily, she had a few *chié* in her pocket and a hollow gourd that she had intended to use on her journey. "I'll mix you something to drink to bring you back to your senses."

María did as she was told. She watched Rosita scoop up some river water and carefully drop in the seeds.

Rosita swirled the mixture. In seconds, the water in the gourd began to thicken. "Here now, take a sip. Only one. Don't spill it."

María took a sip and made a face. "Tastes like spit."

"Too bad. You'll drink some more in another minute."

María sighed. Quietly she asked, "Why don't you help anyone else?"

"What do you mean?"

"People come to the house sometimes. Poor people. Women mostly. They say your mother was a skilled *curandera*. But when they ask for herbs and teas that you must have learned to make from such an accomplished healer, you refuse. Why?"

Rosita scowled. "It is none of your business."

"It is a gift," María persisted in a timid voice.

Rosita tucked her bundle under her arm. "What do you know of gifts? What do you know of anything? I have my reasons. I do not have to share them with anyone as foolish and rude as you. Drink the rest of this. It's time to go back." Abruptly, Rosita motioned for María to stand and follow her up the hill to the path that led back to Guerrero.

María did not budge. "I am sorry I insulted you. Let me make amends. May I sing you a song?"

Rosita impatiently scanned the river. "*Sí*," she said, nodding.

"I'll sing one of the *enlaces*. I plan to perform this song of congratulations for your wedding."

"If you like," Rosita said. She could not hide the dread in her voice. *My wedding.* Now that the boat was gone, how would she ever escape?

María's pure, shining voice cut through the hot air like a knife as she sang "*La Pastora*":

> "*A orillas de un sesteadero*
> *una oveja me faltó,*
> *y una joven blanca y bella*
> *de un pastor se enamoró.*"

> (Close to where the sheep were resting,
> I couldn't find a ewe;
> and a fair and pretty maiden
> fell in love with a shepherd boy.)

While María sang, Rosita forgot about escaping. She simply enjoyed the tune. When María finished, Rosita applauded. "You have a beautiful voice. You should sing loud about daring adventure and heroes so that the whole world can hear you."

María blushed. "I have made up such exciting ballads myself. But you know *corridos* are forbidden to be sung except by men. I would be punished." Whenever she sang at home and sounded the least bit too exuberant, her mother would cover her ears with her soft hands and cry, "*¡Respeto!*" to warn her to keep her tone of respect and sing only in a soft voice — or not at all.

"It's a pity," Rosita replied and began trudging along the path toward the village. María walked beside her. "Why are women not allowed to sing men's songs?"

María wiped sweat from her forehead. "There are rules. How to wear your *rebozo* to enhance your dignity. How to wear your *rebozo* to carry your baby. How to walk through the village. How to speak to your elders. There are rules, you know. Rules for everything." She paused. "What exactly were you doing here by yourself? Mama says there are bandits along the river. And Comanche. And wild animals. This is no place for you. Why did you come here?"

Rosita felt her face flush with anger. Such an annoying, dull, plodding girl! Always following her like a shadow. Always plaguing her with reminders of regulations and traditions. "I don't have to tell you anything," Rosita said with a cold, stony expression. "You are not my real sister. You are nothing. You are — "

Suddenly María gripped Rosita's arm very tightly.

"Let go!" Rosita wriggled free.

María's lips quivered. She pointed with a trembling hand. "Look," she whispered.

Along the bank of the river a coyote with strange

yellow eyes watched them carefully. The tangle of dusty mesquite and other low scrub nearly hid the trickster's dun-colored back, its bushy tail and snub snout. The coyote did not waver. It stood its ground and stared.

And in that moment Rosita knew that she and the coyote carried pictures of each other inside their heads. They had met once before beneath the Sangre de Cristo peaks far to the north when their world had been all fur and fang.

"I am going home," María said fearfully. She fled as fast as she could back to the village.

Rosita did not run. Instead she turned for one last look. The coyote had vanished. Rosita retraced her steps to the river. She searched the riverbank. She was too late again. The coyote was gone.

Just as she was about to walk back to the village, she heard an eerie moaning of something coming around the bend. The noise took her breath away.

The great steamboat!

Part winged, part floating creature, the steamboat was as white and gleaming as a dream. It had two enormous wheels turning on either side like strange, splashing wings that scooped up water. Its single, tall black chimney spit black soot, smoke, and sparks. The boat shrieked and split the brilliant air. When she heard the high, lonesome call of the steamboat, she heard her mother calling, "Flee, Rosita! Flee!"

In a flash she dove behind a mesquite bush and opened her bundle. She wriggled out of her every-day clothing and slipped her expensive, hateful, white wedding dress over her head. She clasped her mother's necklace around her neck and her silk shawl over her shoulders. Without even stopping to think, without even stopping to breathe, she stuffed her castoff skirt, blouse, and shawl under a mesquite bush and stumbled down to the shore of the river. She waved with all her might.

The boat shrieked again. Were her eyes betraying her? The boat was leaving. Rosita waved her shawl over her head. "Stop!" she screamed. "Take me with you!"

The boat gave another terrible howl. A man with bright red hair the color of fire stepped to the top of the boat. He waved back. His face was shockingly pale. Was this the great Señor Austin?

She waved again.

This time she could not believe her eyes. The steamboat stopped. Another smaller boat was low-ered into the water. A man rowed toward her. Unlike the man with the hair the color of fire, this large man was very black. The color of smoke. Rosita felt frozen to the spot.

For the first time she had doubts. *Maybe running away is a mistake.* Maybe she should not go near anything so powerful and mysterious.

Only when the black man smiled and waved, speaking broken Spanish in greeting and gesturing in a friendly way, only then did Rosita break out of her trance. She took one swift look over her shoulder and climbed unsteadily into the little boat.

Chapter

3

María rushed disheveled, face flushed, into the bedroom. Her heart drummed. She dripped with sweat.

"Where have you been?" Frida asked sleepily.
She lifted herself up on one elbow to look at her sister. "You look as though you have seen something
terrible." She sat up and leaned forward eagerly.
"What was it? Tell me."

"Coyote," María said. She gulped. "By the river.
Yellow-eyed and terrible."

Frida frowned. "What were you doing by the
river? You know it is forbidden," she whispered.
"Who was with you?"

"Rosita."

Frida licked her lips. "And what did our dear
stepsister do when she saw the coyote?"

"Ask her yourself. Isn't she here? She was right behind me." María glanced over at Rosita's neatly made bed.

"She has not come back yet," Frida said.

María moaned and covered her face with her hands. "If only I were braver, I never would have left her alone with that coyote. It kept looking and looking at her. As if it knew her."

Frida arched her eyebrows. "As if it *knew* her?"

"I must tell Mama," María said anxiously. "Perhaps she has seen Rosita." She rose to leave, but Frida held her by the arm.

"You need to rest. I will go and talk to Mama. She flies into a temper so easily these days. This is the second time she has had to prepare a wedding feast. You know how she is when she cooks. I will ask if she has seen Rosita."

"You are so kind, Frida," said María, who was not a little afraid of their high-strung mother and her unpredictable rages. "I am very tired."

"Rosita is fine, I'm sure. She's probably taking her time walking back. Don't worry," Frida said. She went to the mirror, combed her hair neatly into a bun, and added a lovely *peineta*. The decorative enamel comb looked charming with her dress, she decided. Don Cassos would think so, too. For good measure, she pinched each of her pudgy, sallow cheeks to give them a bit of color. She glanced at her younger sister, who was already asleep. Softly, Frida left the room, closing the door behind her.

She took a deep breath before making her grand entrance into the kitchen. The sound of pans clattering and spoons banging filled the room. The servants had a familiar battered look as they tiptoed around their mistress, doña Álvarez. Doña Álvarez was a tall, thin woman with proud, dark eyes who liked to remind everyone of her Castilian blood. She was convinced that her Spanish great-great-grandfather had endowed her with superior qualities and therefore she insisted that everyone address her with due respect.

This afternoon she wore a plain apron, her uniform whenever she took command of the kitchen. "The menu again, Octavio. Let me hear you loud and clear this time!" doña Álvarez demanded.

"Bowls of hot chili, plates of tortillas," the timid old servant said. "Roast duck basted in spiced wine and stuffed with meat, piñons and raisins, baked ham, ribs of beef . . . and . . ."

"And what?" doña Álvarez glanced impatiently at Octavio. With a servant like this, how would she ever impress don Cassos?

"I forgot," Octavio murmured. "I am sorry, *señora.*"

"Fresh bread of blue meal, cookies, cakes, and

sweets; beakers of chocolate and flasks of wine. Mussels and flour tortillas. Special egg bread of *hojarasca* to be served with hot chocolate at dawn and at dusk to restore the dancers' energy." Doña Álvarez made an unattractive sputtering noise. "How many times do I have to repeat myself?"

Frida cleared her throat in a suitably humble manner.

"What do you want, Frida? You look like a stupid ewe standing there quivering. Speak up."

"I have something to tell you, Mama," Frida said. She tried to choke down the sense of panic she always experienced in the presence of her critical mother.

"Can't you see I am very busy getting ready for the wedding and feast tomorrow?" Mama stirred a sauce and took a taste with a great wooden spoon. She scowled. "Too salty."

"But, Mama—"

Doña Álvarez rapped the spoon very hard on the edge of the pan. "But Mama what? Speak girl! Stop wasting my time."

"It is about Rosita," Frida said slowly, carefully.

When her mother heard her stepdaughter's name she put down the spoon. She wiped her hands on her apron and took her trembling daughter by the shoulders. "What now?"

Frida gulped. She glanced at the plucked chickens on the table, the piles of elegant sweets arranged on plates, the many delicate sauces bubbling fragrantly in the copper pots and she felt envy flicker and grow in the pit of her stomach like a fire. All this commotion and effort for Rosita, who always treated her with scorn! Rosita, the one who considered herself the most beautiful, the most worthy, the most charming. This wedding was unfair. It should be Frida's turn to be married. She was eldest. Frida took a deep breath. "Mama," Frida said, then paused, "I have come to tell you that Rosita has been deceiving us."

Every servant working in the kitchen stopped to listen.

"What are you saying?" her mother demanded.

Frida lowered her voice. "María saw with her own eyes—by the river." She glanced around the room, all ears upon her. "She said some words. And suddenly a coyote with yellow eyes appeared. The coyote spoke to her. It seemed to know her."

Doña Álvarez gasped. Her hand fluttered to her throat, where she always wore an ornate cross. "Tía Lupe."

Frida bit her lip and nodded. Her eyes seemed to bulge with terror. "Poor María. What if Tía Lupe cast *mal ojo* on her, too? What if Tía Lupe took Rosita with her?"

Doña Álvarez gasped again. She sat on a bench. She never sat down in the kitchen. The sight of their mistress resting amazed the servants so much, they took a few bold steps forward to better hear what Frida and her mother were saying about the evil eye and Rosita and the infamous Tía Lupe.

"Bruja," Octavio murmured wisely.

The other servants nodded in agreement. *"Bruja."*

The possibility of a witch in their midst did not seem outlandish. After all, they had just been visited by a terrifying fire-breathing boat the likes of which no one had ever seen before. Perhaps Tía Lupe's return was somehow connected. Everyone knew that the old woman had been able to magically change from human form into that of a coyote. Everyone knew that when she transformed herself, she left her human eyes behind in a saucer and traveled stealthily around the countryside—usually under cover of darkness. Like all coyotes, her trail of paw prints was always direct, as if she knew exactly where she was going.

Octavio and the other servants glanced nervously toward the open window. Already the sun was beginning to set and the sky was darkening. And still Rosita had not returned.

"Poor, dear don Cassos," Frida said and sniffed loudly. "His heart will be broken."

"If Rosita comes back, we will know the coyote was not Tía Lupe," doña Álvarez reasoned.

"And if she doesn't?" Frida asked and bit her lip.

Doña Álvarez untied her apron. She squared her shoulders. "We must tell your father. We must inform don Cassos. They will know what to do."

Frida dabbed her eyes. For the first time in ever so long, she felt happy.

In the plaza outside the cantina, doña Álvarez spoke to her husband about the terrible news. She described in great detail the coyote with fierce yellow eyes.

"Tía Lupe," don Treviño said and cursed. He should have forbidden his daughter from ever visiting the old woman. Perhaps this tragedy was all his fault.

When don Cassos heard about the disappearance of his bride, his face went pale. He slumped forward in his chair at the cantina.

"I'm sure she'll be home soon," don Treviño told the bridegroom. He hoped he sounded convincing. "She is just a young, headstrong girl. I'm sure she did not mean to insult us both by running away on the eve of her wedding."

Soon everyone in Guerrero had heard the news about Rosita and the yellow-eyed coyote. What did it mean? In detail they discussed Tía Lupe's last words:

"A este pueblo lo maldigo. Terminará bajo las aguas."
Perhaps the fire-breathing steamboat and Rosita's
disappearance had something to do with Tia Lupe's
bizarre curse: "This town will end under the waters."

Villagers argued over what should be done. Some
made the sign of the cross and hid their ears. Others
decided that even if Rosita returned, they would not
attend the wedding or eat any of the Treviño food.
No one could forget the story about the mouse that
had grown in Americus Trinidad's stomach after he
swallowed food touched by a *bruja*. The bewitched
food rumors disturbed proud doña Álvarez most of
all. She could not bear to think that her hard work
and all that food had once again gone to waste.

The crowning blow came early that evening when
Rosita still had not returned. "I am afraid I can
never marry your daughter. Even if she has not been
influenced by an enchanted animal, her disobedient
behavior is most unappealing," don Cassos announced to don Treviño as his wife and two stepdaughters gathered in their home. Don Cassos
glanced at Frida. She smiled back in a particularly
modest and docile manner.

Rosita's father slumped in his chair. He had lost
his first wife and now his precious Rosita, his *charamusca*. He should never have allowed Rosita to visit
Tía Lupe. He should have kept her from the

woman, his wife's only sister. But what could he do? Rosita loved Tía Lupe.

"Don Treviño, are you listening?" doña Álvarez said and tugged on his sleeve. "The *alcade* said the only thing to do is to go to the riverbank and hunt down the coyote. Until they find and kill it, Tía Lupe still roams and no one is safe."

Don Treviño sighed. "And what about Rosita?"

"Don García is gathering a group of villagers to search for her, too," doña Álvarez replied, the authority returning to her voice. "We can only hope they find one coyote, not two."

Don Treviño's shoulders sagged. Reluctantly, he joined the search party made up of the men of Guerrero who were curious or did not wish to be viewed as cowards. The men carried machetes, axes, and knives. Don Cassos, too old to make such a long, difficult walk, sat indoors on a soft chair. He seemed genuinely pleased when Frida remained behind to keep him company. Doña Álvarez also stayed behind to watch over the food.

María did not remain at home. Instead she went along with the search party to describe the coyote in detail and show them where she had last seen her stepsister. She told the story of the coyote so many times, she began to believe that it had truly meant Rosita harm.

"Are you certain of what you saw?" don García asked her as they walked along in the dimming sunlight.

"*Sí,*" she said and bit her lip. She felt so overwhelmed by the idea that Rosita might have been bewitched, she began to sob.

"There, there. Everything will be all right," her stepfather said softly, even though he did not feel the least bit hopeful.

María did not want to believe that Rosita might be gone for good. Such a possibility was far too sad to contemplate. Any moment as she walked among the mesquite she expected to see Rosita larger than life, stepping out, smiling and laughing at them with her loud donkey laughter.

When the group arrived at the Río Bravo, they found no trace of Rosita or the coyote with yellow eyes. Only María's sharp eyes spotted a bit of red fringe from Rosita's *rebozo* clinging to the thorn of a cactus. Don Treviño surveyed the ground. They found the carcass of what looked like a rabbit and a tangle of catfish bones but not one coyote pawprint.

"I am not convinced of this bewitched coyote story," don Treviño said in a mournful voice. "Perhaps Rosita has drowned."

The men spread out along the darkening shore to

search with torches. They found traces of sandal prints that led to the water's edge and vanished. Under a bush one of the searchers found Rosita's crumpled clothing. Don Treviño could not speak. Stunned, he clutched the clothing and stared out over the churning, deep current. Rosita could not swim. If she had gone into the water to swim, she would never make it out again.

For several moments, the other men in the search party could not think of what to say, what to do. They believed that Rosita had not gone swimming. No. They believed she must have slipped out of her clothing when she, too, changed into the form of a second coyote.

Don García nervously cleared his throat. "Don Treviño, we can do nothing more now," he said. Clouds covered the moon that was nearly full. In the light of the villagers' torches ghostly mesquite danced and quivered. Don García and the others were nervous to go home to make sure nothing had happened to their families. Searching for signs of a *bruja* was dangerous and risky. María, too, felt anxious to return to the safety of the village.

"Are you coming back with us?" don García asked.

Don Treviño shook his head. María and the villagers walked back to Guerrero while don Treviño wandered up and down the riverbank calling his daughter's name. Hours later he stumbled home again, devastated that Rosita had vanished.

Out of earshot of her father, some villagers gossiped that they were lucky to be rid of Rosita. They complained of her violin playing and her strange, restless spirit.

"She will never make anyone a good wife," some said. "Just the other day I saw her flying over a cornfield."

"I spotted her peering in our window."

"The river may never give up her body," others agreed. "What do all these strange signs mean?"

"Dark days ahead."

Disgusted by such talk, María left the search party and shuffled into the house. She went to the bedroom and looked through Rosita's belongings, wondering how they should decorate her grave. *Her violin.* This thought filled María with sadness. She had always liked to hear Rosita play. Now she'd never hear her again.

She searched all the hiding places where she knew Rosita kept the violin. She found nothing. This puzzled María for a few minutes. She shut her eyes and tried to recall how her stepsister had looked the last time she saw her. She had been standing on the path back to Guerrero, looking irritated and clutching something protectively in her arms. A *morral*. Inside that woven bag was something Rosita clearly did not want her to see.

What was it?

Suddenly, she knew.

The violin.

María took a deep breath. Rosita would have taken the violin with her for only one reason — she was running away. And someone as extraordinary as Rosita would never escape in an ordinary way. María smiled. She remembered the footprints that ended at the river's edge. They, too, could mean only one thing.

Rosita must have vanished on the fire-breathing steamboat.

Chapter 4

Rosita sat quietly, gripping the sides of the little scow as it was rowed through the current toward the ship. Two rough-looking men grabbed the line thrown to them by the black man, tied up the scow, and offered their hands to help her with her bag on to the steamboat. She gulped and stepped aboard. The steamboat seemed to throb like a thing alive. Cows lowed on the deck. A pig scurried past, pursued by a boy. The sound of loud humming, punctuated by an ominous *boom-boom-boom* made it hard to speak loud enough for anyone to hear her.

She held tight to her bundle in the *morral* as she tried to steady herself against the white railing. The boat dipped and rolled. No one else seemed bothered by the strange movement. A family perched on two bales of cotton stared at her. The man and woman looked at her with sullen, sunken eyes. Their children, three dirty, barefoot boys and a baby, gnawed on pieces of stale hardtack. Rosita smiled at them and tried to make a little curtsy. They said something unfriendly sounding in English. She looked away. *Well, I'll just have to make the best of the situation.*

The black man signaled to her to follow him past the cattle and the machinery and the boxes and barrels and crates stored everywhere. The boat had a clumsy, makeshift look. There was little of grace or dignity about it, she thought. It towered awkwardly above the water like a wooden house floating on a flat raft. From a distance the wood had gleamed white. Up close she could see where the paint was peeling and pulling away. Wood trim had been hastily cut into ornate designs and tacked up to cover the edges of the stairway. When she touched one slivered section, it bent in her hand.

"Señorita?" the man said to her and smiled. He showed her how to walk around a line of laundry and a cow that was being milked. The place smelled of animals and unwashed humans and greasy food. The floor was slick with water, hay, and manure. She tried not to breathe through her nose. How many people were on this boat? She couldn't tell.

Twenty? Thirty? Forty? She counted heads that appeared and then disappeared. No one greeted her. No one seemed particularly pleased to see her. The other passengers examined her with bored disinterest.

The whole deck felt hot, as if a great fire were burning someplace. The floor vibrated with the same strange thrumming beat she had felt earlier. It was especially loud and strong now. Fear twisted in her stomach. *Where is he taking me?*

They passed one of the churning paddle wheels, which was as tall as the finest house in Guerrero. As the wheel turned each slat slapped the water and dripped when it came out of the water. The wheel turned inside what looked like a partially covered box. She followed the black man up a set of stairs that climbed up to a second level. Here the noise was not so terrible, the smell not so strong and the heat less oppressive.

A balcony surrounded the second level all the way around the boat. The black man opened a door for her and she entered what seemed to be a long, narrow room. The only light came from a single window above where a group of men smoking cigars was intent on a card game. At either end of the room was a mirror. All along the walls were ornately carved doors. She wondered where they went.

In the growing darkness of late afternoon the room seemed magnificent. She ran a hand over a red chair that was remarkably soft. Nearby was a rocking chair and a sofa. The carpeting was thick beneath her feet. Overhead the ceiling was painted in gleaming colors with angels staring down at her. She thought of church. The villagers' stories had been correct. Not even Nuestra Señora del Refugio was as elegant as this place. Rosita felt as if she must be dreaming. Such a dazzling boat! She was speechless with wonder.

The black man kept walking. He finally stopped outside a door and knocked. A red-faced man with a bulging stomach opened the door. His desk was covered with books and pieces of paper. He quickly put on his jacket when he saw Rosita standing there. He made a short bow and spoke in excellent Spanish. *"Buenos días, señorita,"* he said in greeting. His eyes were close set and bloodshot. He looked like a worried man, like a man who saw ghosts. "My name is Mr. Albert Oliver. I am delighted that you have decided to join us on our trip south."

Rosita murmured her thanks. Before she could introduce herself, a bell clanged loudly.

"I suggest you hold on to a solid object, *señorita,*" he said quickly and braced himself against his desk.

In seconds the entire boat shuddered and groaned as it slammed against something.

Rosita let out a little scream of fright. She was hurtled against a wall and knocked a book from the desk. She righted herself and her belongings. "What is that? Are we sinking?" she demanded anxiously.

"No, no, ma'am. Just a pesky sandbar. Nothing to concern your pretty little head about," Oliver said with great confidence, even though his own plump hands shook. "Now about your fare—"

Captain Austin stuck his head inside the clerk's office and exploded in English, "What kind of cussedness is this? Can the man steer the boat neither drunk nor sober?" When he saw Rosita, he blushed. "Sorry, ma'am," he said apologetically.

"Another passenger," Oliver said. He opened a drawer and poured himself a great capful of patent medicine from a green-tinted bottle.

"Delighted to meet you," Captain Austin said and removed his hat, revealing his thinning hair. He spoke Spanish in a modest, shy manner. "I hope you will be comfortable on our voyage. It is delightful to have such a lady of distinction aboard. Are you going far?"

Rosita did not know what to say. She had not considered how far she would travel. All she knew was that she wanted to go far enough that no one would try to come to find her and bring her back to Guerrero again. Uncertain, she did what she always did around shy, bumbling men. She smiled a winning, devastating smile.

Captain Austin blushed. "We go . . . we go as far as Matamoros."

"Matamoros," she said sweetly. "That is where I wish to go."

Captain Austin replaced his hat. "Would you like to see *Ariel?*"

She wasn't sure who Ariel was. She decided to please him, however, and nodded. He motioned for her to follow him. *"Ariel* has great speed and power," Captain Austin said proudly. "She can run as fast as seven knots an hour."

Seven knots. What does he mean? Rosita smiled. "Faster than a horse?"

He chuckled. "Much faster."

Can such a woman exist? Rosita wondered.

"She carries one hundred thousand pounds of freight and here is where she burns wood in her great furnaces," he continued. They paused before roaring ovens that boomed and threw off terrible heat. The same black man who had rowed her in the scow now stood beside the furnace. He leaned against a pole, his exhausted face streaked with sweat, and watched Captain Austin warily.

Captain Austin continued, "These furnaces are what makes her bulge amidships."

Rosita nodded again, feeling more confused than ever. Ariel was very fat, very fast, and needed to be constantly kept very warm. Surely this fat, fast Texas woman who could not stand the cold must be a wonder. Perhaps she was Austin's wife. It did seem comely for her husband to speak of her strange qualities with such admiration, though. Perhaps these Texas men did not think of their women with the same kind of respect that the men of Guerrero did.

"She takes a draft of between three and four feet of water," Captain Austin said with growing enthusiasm.

"Three and four feet?" Rosita said with astonishment. "Is it possible for a woman to drink so much?"

Captain Austin laughed as they climbed back up the steps again. "Ah, you are droll! It is wonderful to have such a charming lady aboard. I trust you will find your cabin room on the *Ariel* adequate." He stood outside a door and motioned for her entry. Then she understood. *Ariel* was the name of the boat.

She looked inside the small room he called a cabin. It was six feet square with two bunks built into one wall. She felt the bed and was relieved to see that it was soft, although the linens were far coarser than those at home.

"These are our best accommodations. As for your payment," he said, pausing. "I hope that you will not find our fare of ten dollars unreasonable. This includes your meals. We have had few ladies of your distinction as passengers."

Ten dollars! She had not thought to bring even one peso. All she had was what she was wearing and what she carried in her arms.

"You are going all the way to Matamoros," he said quickly. "That is our farthest destination."

She felt his eyes inspecting her mother's necklace. Protectively she put a hand up to her neck. *Not this.* She sensed that he might change his mind about taking her as a passenger. *What if he makes me get off the boat?* Surely he would not let her travel for free. He was a *gringo*, she knew. And she knew enough about these strangers from conversations she had overheard with her father and other men from the village to know that the one thing they wanted and admired was money. She would have to come up with a plan to pay Captain Austin in some way, somehow. She would think of a plan. She needed time.

"Certainly, I understand your fare," she said in

her most charming voice. "You must understand that in my village we often bargain for what we buy. Please do not take offense. I can see this is something that you do not do in your country." She smiled in a most fetching manner and lifted her silk *rebozo* up around her shoulders.

For the first time she realized what an effect her fine wedding clothing was having on the *norteamericano*. He considered her a very rich lady because of her dress and jewelry. *So be it. Let him consider me so for a little while longer.* "And if you will please excuse me, I would like to rest for a little while," she said and motioned for him to exit so that she could close the door behind him.

Dazzled once more by her charm, he removed his hat briefly. "And may I have the pleasure of knowing your name, ma'am?"

"Rosita Ana Trinidad Gutiérrez Alonzo Treviño," Rosita said with elegant completeness, using all her names — even the ones she seldom mentioned.

Captain Austin seemed impressed. He stumbled backward and disappeared.

Rosita shut the door. Carefully she unwrapped the bundle from inside the woven bag. Tía Lupe's old violin and bow. This was not worth ten dollars. The only possession which might pay her fare was her necklace. But how could she part with it? It was all she had left to remind her of her mother. She had to think of something. Something else she could barter.

She felt the floor shudder beneath her feet and remembered that the boat was moving. Even as she had stood here speaking to that foolish captain, the boat was carrying her toward freedom. With every passing moment she was moving farther and farther away from Guerrero.

Rosita could not help herself. She smiled.

Chapter

5

That evening in Guerrero the servants in the Treviño home refused to venture outdoors. "What if the bewitched coyote appears?" Octavio demanded. He and the other servants drew the shutters closed and kept watch by the door, terrified of spotting a *bruja* flying in a fireball or an egg. No one dared go outside in the night. Too many strange and bizarre things had occurred. The great fire-breathing ship on the river The disappearance of the bride. The news of Tía Lupe come back disguised as a coyote. It was all too disturbing. Better stay inside and be safe.

Meanwhile, don Cassos remained as an honored guest. He seemed to suffer badly from the gout and decided he could not travel back to his hacienda so soon. He retreated to the best bed in the house. Frida, delighted to show her abilities as a nurse, fluttered about him.

"Don Cassos, isn't Frida a wonder?" ever-hopeful doña Álvarez said. She was delighted when the old man nodded eagerly.

Rosita's father, filled with despair, locked himself in the family chapel and would not come out. He felt certain that it was something he had said that caused his Rosita, his precious only daughter, to abandon reason and abandon him.

As the full moon rose higher in the night sky, no one paid any attention to María. She sat in a corner of the kitchen and imagined how her days would stretch ahead in a kind of sameness as blank and pale as the baked earth. How quiet and boring life would be without Rosita!

María was like the moon. She reflected Rosita's glory. She basked in the admiring glances that came her stepsister's way and imagined everyone saying to themselves, "Oh, she is the stepsister. Isn't she lucky?" She secretly marveled at Rosita's boldness, her quick tongue, her expressions of disdain and donkey laughter—delight that she could never express. With Rosita gone María felt as if life had ended. All hope had vanished. Rosita was the only one who had ever given her genuine encouragement to sing. "You have a beautiful voice," she had told her.

Remembering those words made María want to sing. Softly, she sang the first melody that sprang to her lips.

"Ahí vienen los inditos
por el carrizal,
ahí veinen los inditos
por el carrizal.
¡Ay mamita! ¡ay papito!
me quieren matar,
¡ay mamita! ¡ay papito!
me quieren matar.
Ahí vienen los inditos
por el carrizal."

(The little Indians are coming
through the canebrake,
the little Indians are coming
through the canebrake,
Oh, mommy! Oh, daddy!
They want to kill me.
Oh, mommy! Oh, daddy!
They want to kill me.
The little Indians are coming
through the canebrake.)

"Stop that horrible song," her mother commanded. "No one wants to hear about little Indians coming through the canebrake to kill somebody."

"It is only a harmless baby-bouncing song," María said sadly. "You used to sing it to us, remember?"

Her mother put her fists on her hips. "You are a selfish, inconsiderate girl. Can't you see how ill don Cassos is? The servants are wild with fear and your stepfather is mourning inconsolably. No one wants to hear such disturbing music. I forbid you to sing."

María looked at her mother in astonishment. "You forbid me to sing for the rest of the evening?"

Angrily, her mother opened her fan and surveyed the half-cooked food, the dirty pots and pans, the filthy kitchen. She took a deep breath and fluttered the fan in front of her flushed face. It would take days to restore order. And how would she accomplish anything with her mutinous servants and her worthless husband? She was glad his precious Rosita was gone. She had always been trouble. Good riddance. Now perhaps her Frida would have a chance.

"Mama?" María demanded. "Did you hear what I just asked?"

"*¡Ay mija!*" her mother exclaimed impatiently. "Oh, child! What now?"

"Do you mean this evening or forever?"

Doña Álvarez picked up a pan caked with *frijoles*.

The refried beans were hard and burned. Such a waste! "Forever! Forever!" doña Álvarez exclaimed angrily. She dropped the pot. It clattered against the floor.

María jumped to her feet. Tears sprang to her eyes. She would not stay here without Rosita. She would not stay here if she could not sing.

"Where are you going?" her mother demanded. She rolled up her sleeves and tossed two blackened pans into a tub of water.

"Nowhere," María mumbled. *I will run away. Tonight.*

"Go and help your sister. See if there is anything don Cassos needs."

María stomped out of the kitchen, but she did not go to her sister. *No one watches me. No one pays attention. No one will even notice I am gone.* She felt as if the floor under her had opened up with a terrifying wave of pity, whispering, "Let go!"

She would find Rosita. They would escape on the steamboat together and see the ocean. *This time she will be glad to see me.*

María knew it would be too dangerous to travel as a girl. Someone could recognize her and force her to go home. She recalled a story she had read about a brave girl who disguised herself as a boy to travel to a distant kingdom. She would do that, too. "I am not brave but I can certainly find a disguise."

She found on the laundry line some of the clothing of a servant boy who had been given fine trousers and a serape for the wedding to impress don Cassos. She took a pair of scissors from her sister's sewing basket and hacked away at her hair. *Snip-snip-snip.* She threw her hair out the window under a pomegranate tree and did not feel the least bit sad. Her hair was always a bother—always in her face. Not much to look at. Not as beautiful as Frida's and certainly not as lovely as Rosita's. She was glad to see it disappear. Having her hair cut short made her feel like a new person. A person she did not recognize when she looked into the mirror. She felt more courageous already.

She tucked her grandfather's book of poetry into her serape and slipped out of the house. No one noticed María dash toward the river. In the moonlight she could see the path ahead with no difficulty. The air smelled sweet and dusty and promising. Wind cooled her face. She walked faster, humming in a steady jogging tempo.

"Desde esa ciudad de Jauja
me mandan solicitar,
que me vaya para allá
un tesoro a disfrutar."

(They have sent from that city
of Jauja, asking for me;
They want me to go there,
so I may enjoy a treasure.)

Soon she came to the roiling Río Bravo gleaming in the moonlight. Mesquite shadows shifted. Thorny shrubs grumbled. This was as far as María had ever wandered from home. She knew she had to head south, the direction the steamboat was going. She gulped. Something scrambled furiously over the dry ground. Then the low keening cry of an animal. A hidden owl called ominously, "*¡Tú! ¡Tú!*" which sounded to María like, "You! You!"

María shivered. She thought of the story Rosita had once told her about phantom children who played near the river. Perhaps they were lingering nearby, watching her at this very moment. Her heart beat in her throat. *Maybe I should go home.* She turned and retraced a few steps, then stopped. She ran a hand through her shorn hair and glanced down quickly at her stolen clothes. Immediately, she imagined what would happen when she returned—her mother's angry scowl and Frida's scornful, black lizard eyes.

No, she knew she would have to be brave and keep going. Rosita had gone before her. She had escaped. María decided that she could do the same. To keep up her courage she trotted along and chanted.

*"Arroyos que corren leche,
jarros y cazos de atole,
hay barrancas de panochas,
hay azúcar con pinole."*

(There are creeks that flow with milk;
pots and kettles of *atole;*
there are mounds of brown sugar;
there is sugar with *pinole.*)

Singing of a fantastic place with creeks that flowed with milk, pots and kettles of gruel made of boiled corn meal, mounds of brown sugar, and sugar with toasted corn ground to a fine powder gave her strength to move forward down the river. *Who knows what marvelous things we'll find when we reach the ocean?*

Suddenly she stopped. She sniffed. Smoke. Someone burning mesquite? She peered in the distance. The flicker of a campfire. Desperate, she dropped to her knees, squeezed her eyes shut, and listened as hard as she could. Comanche? No. Someone spoke Spanish in a low voice. Another low voice answered. Two men arguing in a drunken slur. She did not recognize their voices or understand what they were saying. *Who are they?* For several moments, she was too terrified to move, too terrified to breathe. *What if they're bandits?*

She wished she were home again, safe and sound. Back in her dull, boring house where nothing ever happened and no one ever noticed her.

"*Cabeza de puerco!*" one voice shouted. "Double crosser! Liar! Cheat!"

"You think you are the *camandulero!* So sly, so cunning, so treacherous. Why didn't you kill that *vaquero* when you had the chance? All this trouble for that cowboy's little bag of pesos. Hardly enough to buy a round of decent drinks."

"Are you accusing me of being a coward?"

"*Sí!*"

For the next several moments she heard the unmistakable sound of *una pelez furiosa.* The bandits were settling things by fighting. They tossed each other against the prickly cactus and hollered and stumbled and butted each other with their heads. She heard hard thuds and the skitter of gravel and sand, the grunts and blunt blows of staggering men fighting. Just as she was about to sneak past them along the riverbank where the shadows were thickest and they would not notice her, the scuffling stopped.

She froze.

All was silent except for the hoarse sound of heavy breathing. Someone belched.

"You—you saw the boat on the river," a loud voice announced. "Tomorrow we attack with our new rifles. There must be plenty of gold on board that *norteamericano* boat. Picking them off will be as easy as deer hunting."

"No more hanging back, you *alburuzero*. This time we will be rich men."

"*¡Alburuzero!* Who are you calling a noisy boaster?"

María crouched on the ground, uncertain what to do next. Rosita would be in terrible danger if the boat were attacked. Somehow María knew she had to warn Señor Austin. But if she tried to creep past the bandits now, they would certainly see her. She had to think of a plan. As carefully as she could, she scrambled closer to the river. Her heel slipped. Rocks rolled.

"What was that?" one of the bandits demanded.

"I didn't hear anything."

The air filled with the eerie, mournful song of a woman. A loud voice echoed along the river bank:

"Viene la muerte y quedaremos igualitos,
en este mundo todo tiene su hasta aquí."

"Now I heard it for sure," one bandit whispered.

"Go look," his companion replied.

"Not me. Did you hear what she's singing?"

" 'Death will come, and we will all be the same, for in this world everything comes to an end.' "

For several moments the bandits were silent.

"*La Llorena!* What else can it be? Roaming the river, looking for her drowned children."

Now their voices were filled with terror. "*¡Cuela!* Let's get out of here!"

In their haste to escape the ghost of the tormented woman called *La Llorena,* the bandits did not notice María hiding in the shadows. They quickly saddled their horses and galloped away. The dust moved down the path like a ghost.

María rose slowly. She glanced with relief in each direction and resumed her journey down the bank of the Río Bravo.

Nearly a league later she spotted the *Ariel* floating in the middle of the current. In the moonlight the boat looked bigger and whiter and more terrifying than anything she had imagined. How could she ever reach it? Once again she wondered if she should turn back.

She squinted at the illuminated windows. The boat seemed bewitched. Or maybe it was her eyes. Somewhere looking out at the moon she thought she spied Rosita. Perhaps her eyes were deceiving her. For a very long time she sat on a log on the muddy shore near the protection of a pile of slimy driftwood. Mosquitoes buzzed in her ears. She hoped she could not easily be seen by anyone looking down at the river from the bluff. Wearily, she leaned her chin on her fist, her elbow on her knee. *What if the bandits come back?* She did not know what to do.

She must have dozed, hunched over. *Splash!* Her head snapped up. In the river she heard the sound of men's voices, of paddles. A *chalana*, like the kind she had seen on the Río Salado, crossed the moonlit river. Someone held a bright lantern aloft. A low voice sang in English words she did not understand. The mournful song kept rhythm with the sound the water made against the oars. *Norteamericanos.*

Carefully, she crept in the shadows and watched the three men climb out of the boat and walk heavily into a stand of trees. She could only see their backs as they lumbered into the dense scrub. Two of them carried axes; the third man had what looked like a rifle slung over his shoulder. Soon she heard the sound of chopping.

The men worked quickly and quietly, seldom speaking to each other. Branches of ebony and willow and mesquite were hurled into a pile. The man with the lantern walked to the shore. Holding the lantern aloft he moved it up and down several times as if he were signaling.

Slowly, the great steamboat began to move. It roared, louder and louder. The great glittering boat seemed to be lit up brighter than a thousand novena candles. At the very top of this marvelous, illuminated boat she saw a smaller room. A lonely silhouette looked out like some great-eyed god. *Can he see me?* She dodged behind a pile of driftwood.

Spellbound, she watched the great boat grow. The noise seemed deafening. It shuddered and wheezed and made growling and groaning noises as it headed straight for the shore. She expected at any moment to hear the boat splinter and crash against the trees, against the shore and then climb out of the water on its own legs.

But the great boat did none of these things. Instead, at the last possible moment, the roaring stopped. The great dripping, paddling noise ceased. Men shouted. The ground beneath her bare feet trembled as the boat nosed into the soft mud of the shore.

"Wood-pile, wood-pile, where are the wooders?" someone sang out in melodic Spanish then in English.

There was a great clattering as planks were lowered from the ship to the shore. And from the great belly of the ship came two more men. They yawned and spoke in complaining voices as they walked across the planking into the woods. *Where are they going? What are they doing?*

María crept closer. Suddenly, she felt the ground thud with heavy footsteps. Her heart beat wildly. Before she could dart into the shadows a large, strong hand grabbed her roughly by the shoulder and held her tight.

Chapter

6

"What have we got here?" a voice boomed in English. "Looks like a new deckhand to me."

What is he saying? Frantically, María twisted. McCallister's face was covered by a shadow. With all her might she tried to wriggle free. "*Señor*, let me go," she pleaded in Spanish. "I bring you news. A pair of *banditos* with rifles. You are in great danger. Let me come aboard. Let me speak to the great and powerful Captain Austin."

"You go-long now! Can't understand a word you say. *Banditos?* Guess I know that one. What's this fellow saying about *banditos*, Carlos?" McCallister demanded. That was all they needed. They had run aground eleven times and lost one crew member

from drowning. In nearly one week they had traveled only sixty miles.

Carlos, a skinny Mexican deckhand who looked
to be perhaps thirteen, peered at María over the
pile of wood he carried in his arms. "This stranger
says there are two bandits upriver waiting to
attack," he translated for McCallister.

"Two?" McCallister scoffed. "Hardly worth
bothering about. This fellow got a name? Got a reason for being here in the middle of the night? How
do we know he ain't a bandit?"

"*¿Como se llama?*" Carlos asked kindly.

"José," María replied. She hoped she sounded
convincing when she explained that she was head-
ing south alone and wished to journey on the great
boat.

"Have you got any money?" Carlos asked.

María shook her head. She had no money but
told him that she was willing to work to pay her
fare. Carlos grinned.

"José just signed on as a deckhand, *señor,*" Carlos
said.

"Good," McCallister replied. "Get to work."

Carlos handed her a pile of wood and branches.
"Carry these on to the ship."

María felt her arms strain, her knees buckle.
Carry them? How? Her back ached. But she tried not

to show she was not strong enough. One by one the men shouldered the wood over the plank to the boat. The narrow plank wobbled. Ten feet below flowed dark water. María gulped. She tried not to look down as she made her way slowly across the plank. She tried not to think what would happen if she fell in and was swept away.

"Hurry up!" someone shouted behind her.

She gulped. A chunk of wood from her arms fell into the water. *Splash!* She slipped and caught her balance. Only a few more feet. A few more. Perspiration ran down her face. Biting flies droned around her bare arms, her neck. One more step. She staggered on to the boat and dumped the wood all over the deck.

"Pick it up! Pick it up!" McCallister bellowed. She felt a menacing thump on the floor. When she looked up she saw a long hickory stick raised over her head. Instinctively, she closed her eyes and shielded her face.

A low voice growled in English. She felt someone brush against her arm. When she opened her eyes, she spied black hands quickly picking up the wood. An enormous man, one of the pair she had seen on the little boat, knelt beside her helping to gather up her wood. The hickory stick was gone. So was McCallister.

María's hands trembled as she stacked the wood. *"Gracias, señor,"* she said to the large black man.

He did not answer. His glance told her nothing. She wondered who he was and what his name was.

For the next hour the wooding party, including María, chopped and carried six cords of fuel from the shore to the boat. The embankment was nearly twenty feet high. And between the plank and the level embankment was a long patch of slimy mud that made walking dangerous and slippery.

María was exhausted when they were finally finished, she staggered on to the deck. The planking was drawn back into the ship. Carlos smiled at her. "Not too bad, was it?" he asked.

She was too tired to answer.

"If you're traveling deck passage, you sleep over here. Anywhere you can find a space," Carlos said. He pointed to the places where whole families were curled among the bales and boxes and barrels. In the darkness she smelled horses and cows — the smells of a barnyard.

"Ow!" someone complained. "Watch where you walk!"

"Lo siento," María said. She could barely see the people stretched out on the hard surface of the boat.

"This is where I sleep," Carlos said. By the light

of the ship's torch she could see how he had arranged a few gunnysacks and a bit of straw and used a ragged blanket to cover himself. Carlos, who had grown up in Laredo where he had no place to sleep and seldom ate a meal a day, felt pleased to be aboard a boat where he was housed, fed, and paid regularly. He was seeing the world. And he had his own bag of money, which he kept tied around his neck. He felt like a rich man.

"This is your bed?" María asked with disbelief. She thought of her soft bed at home.

"The deckhands sleep wherever they can," he said. "This is a very good spot. It's as far from the boilers as you can be and still have a bit of roof over your head. You do not want to be too close to the boiler because it can blow up. Explode. *Boom.*" He made a loud, satisfied exploding noise with his mouth.

"The boiler? What is that?" María asked nervously.

"The boiler makes the fire that runs the ship. Tomorrow you will see."

María did not think she really wanted to see the boiler. She did not really think she wanted to stay on this dangerous boat that smelled of manure and rattled and might blow up at any moment. *Where is Rosita?* How would she find her?

María was too tired to think, too tired to do any-thing but thankfully accept Carlos's offer of a gun-nysack. She curled up on the grimy, splintered planking of the deck next to the woodpile with her serape wrapped around her book. She lay her head on the serape and closed her eyes. In a moment she was sound asleep.

The next morning Rosita awoke and wondered if she were home again. She blinked hard and sat up. Had she dreamed she heard María's voice? What an irritating dream. She did not wish to think of her annoying stepsister. Not today. Not on the first day of her great journey.

Outside her cabin door she heard someone argu-ing in English. She wished she could understand what they were saying. Suddenly there was a knock. *"Señorita?"* a low voice demanded. *"Desayuno."*

Rosita dressed hurriedly for breakfast. She could already feel the ship rattle and hum, punctuated every now and again by an explosive burst of exhaust. The constant creaking, groaning, and pounding was louder than the falls of El Salto back home. She looked out the little window, wiped the dirty pane of glass with her finger, and saw the trees moving. She was traveling! The boat was moving and she suddenly felt filled with hope and expectation. She opened the door a crack and saw a great table in the middle of the saloon that had not been there the night before. The odor of greasy fried meat filled the air and she could hear someone shouting and pans clanging. She crossed the saloon to a small door that she had been shown by Captain Austin. He called it something odd. *A water closet.* What could that mean? Perhaps a place to wash her face. She had to keep up appearances. This was her only dress. She wanted to seem presentable. A real lady.

Inside the small room a pinch-faced Mexican woman was scrubbing the face of her young son. A few tin basins with pitchers of cloudy river water were set out on a bench with a common towel roller, a community comb with glittering hair stuck to it and a battered community toothbrush. Rosita tried not to look disgusted as she asked the woman if she knew where the toilet facilities were located.

"Over there," Madame de la Barca said. She was traveling with her son and maid. The haughty woman pointed down the way to another door that led to a very filthy outhouse built into the wheel-house. The openings of the primitive toilets emptied directly into the river. Rosita waved a hand in front of her face, exited, and quickly closed the door.

By now the saloon was filling with sleepy-looking cabin passengers. Rosita recognized the "river sharper," or gambler, from the night before. He spoke to no one but quickly took his seat and poured himself some coffee. Reverend Spike, a tall, thin man with a high collar, sat across from him. A handful of quiet men traveling together sat down at the other end. They looked tired and dusty and they wore their spurs and hats at the table. Madame de la Barca sat with her whining son and disgruntled maid at the far end of the table. Rosita, not knowing where to sit, took her place on a bench beside a Texan with a drooping moustache stained with tobacco juice.

She wanted to speak to someone, to find out where they were from and where they were going, but no one seemed interested in conversation. As soon as a harried-looking man brought in platters of beefsteak, cooked pigeon, chicken fricassee, and plates of cold sliced ham of a slightly suspicious green color, the entire group began to eat with a furious sense of purpose.

Rosita watched fascinated and appalled as the group chewed and cut and sliced and grabbed and chewed some more. They ate fiercely, silently—not once passing the food. *"Buenos días,"* she said politely to the Texan.

He grunted and grabbed another piece of pigeon.

Reverend Spike, with elbows out, expertly speared pieces of beefsteak into his mouth using the tip of his knife. The preacher made loud sucking noises as he raised the knife to his mouth and vacuumed off the food that did not fall into his lap. The quiet, dusty men in spurs bent over their plates and shoveled food directly into their mouths. Neither Madame de la Barca nor her maid did anything to stop the young boy from smearing the best part of a spoonful of cooked, gelatinous pigeon everywhere.

By the time Rosita politely asked to be passed some meat, everything except the greenish ham was gone. No one had dared to touch the ham. Rosita's stomach growled as she sipped bitter, lukewarm coffee. She thought of the lovely way her stepmother's cook prepared delicious hot chocolate for her. And for the first time she felt a swift, brief pang of homesickness.

Captain Austin, who was late in sitting down at the head of the table, greeted the group with a good-natured smile. He carried a plate of what appeared to be boiled potatoes. Everyone looked up at once. "Found these in the pilothouse," he said in a jovial manner.

The passengers immediately began to grumble.

"Captain, you advertised rice, corn with rice pudding, and special French tarts and numerous other rare desserts with dinner for first-class passage," Madame de la Barca said in an accusing manner. "We have yet to see any of these delicacies at this table. All we have been served is meat, meat, and more meat. Badly prepared and of dubious quality. Of milk and butter there is none. This goes hard on the delicate stomach of a sensitive child, Captain Austin." She glanced with concern at her greasy-faced son, who was busy painting himself with gravy.

"Now, ma'am," Captain Austin said and chewed with exuberance. "We will be having those European delicacies heaps of times once we get near a town where supplies can be procured. Yes, ma'am, my chef will make any kind of pastry your heart desires."

"Sir, when exactly will we be arriving in Matamoros?" the gambler asked in a low, lizard-like voice. "On the same advertisement you promised a swift trip. Fastest journey on the Río Grande. A lame man could walk more swiftly than we've traveled. We have visited every sandbar, every snag. We have taken near an eternity to travel two hundred miles."

Captain Austin quickly finished his potatoes and began elaborately picking his teeth with an ivory toothpick he produced from his vest pocket. "Sir, this is no dull cart-horse sort of boat, useful for the meanest kind of work. This is an exploratory craft. We are going where no steamboat has ventured before. On such a historic voyage you cannot expect top speed. No, sir."

The gambler did not look satisfied by this explanation. He belched, pushed himself back from the table. Rosita did not like the way his dark eyes inspected her necklace before he made his way to the far end of the saloon, where he began to noisily shuffle his trusty pack of cards. Just as the rest of the cabin-class passengers were about to leave the table, a shot rang out. Then another.

Madame de la Barca screamed. The other passengers dove under the table. Rosita, not knowing what to do, sat frozen in her seat.

Chapter 7

"Take cover!" Captain Austin shouted. He leapt to his feet and raced for the pilothouse, the small room at the very top of the ship. "Mr. Rackliffe!"

A bell clanged. From the deck below came shouts and screams. Animals lowed, bellowed, and yowled. Crew members clambered up and down the stairs. They shoved deck passengers out of their way and shouted to others to hide behind bales and boxes.

More shots rang out. Glass from a window splintered all over the floor.

"Where's it coming from this time?" Captain Austin shouted to McCallister.

"Across the river, near the port bow. Snipers in the trees," McCallister replied. He was already loading the cannon with help from a terrified deck-hand. "Permission to fire, sir?"

"Permission granted," Captain Austin replied.

The whole ship seemed to shake when the blast went off. Smoke filled the air. Trees across the river crumpled.

Rosita, who had finally crawled under the table with the rest of the cabin passengers, felt as if she might be sick. The air filled with the smell she remembered when fireworks went off at fiesta time. *What is happening? Will we all be killed?*

Madame de la Barca's little boy was crying. The preacher mumbled some prayers. Only the gambler, who was an experienced steamboat traveler, kept laying out the cards on the table as if nothing at all were happening. After several moments no more gunfire was heard. Bells rang. The steam whistle sounded. And there was a great blast of exhaust from the chimney overhead. The boat lurched forward.

Captain Austin tramped into the saloon triumphantly. The rest of the cabin passengers crawled reluctantly out from under the table. *"Banditos,"* he announced. "They won't be back. You can be sure of that. We scared them completely."

"Señor, was anyone . . . anyone injured?" Rosita asked from under the table.

"Just a few folks belowdecks," Captain Austin replied. "Nothing to worry about."

The rest of the cabin passengers went about their business. Rosita was the last to crawl out from under the table. Her legs shook. She looked around and saw the spot where the bullet had entered the saloon. The wall was as thin and flimsy as a piece of paper. For the first time she noticed the cheapness of the saloon's flaking woodwork. What had seemed luxurious in dim light, by day appeared quite shabby. The chair arms had been whittled with knives by bored passengers and the red upholstery sagged greasy black in places. Grime coated the mirrors. The angels on the ceiling had peeling faces and the carpeting was worn through in spots.

"Perhaps I may be of some assistance, *señor,*" Rosita said. She brushed off her dress and straightened her silk *rebozo*. "Someone is hurt?"

"Now don't you worry your pretty little head about those folks," Captain Austin said.

"It's no bother, *señor,*" Rosita insisted. She did not like the way he kept staring at her necklace. As soon as she returned to her cabin she would hide it someplace safe. "I would be happy to take a look at any injuries. Although I do not have any supplies with me, I have some experience. You see, my mother—"

"Fine, fine," Captain Austin said impatiently. A bell was ringing urgently from the pilothouse. "I must go."

Rosita crept down the stairs to the main deck, which was filled with noise and confusion and terrible smells. A pig had escaped and was tearing through the boxes and bales dragging a line of laundry. A boy shouted and chased the pig. A hungry baby cried in its mother's arms. Another little girl hobbled past.

She had not realized how many people were packed into the place with so much cargo. The sight of so much suffering overwhelmed her. What could she do? She was only one person. She quickly retraced her steps back up to the cabin level, went to her room, and shut the door.

That evening Rosita heard a sharp rap at her door. Quickly, she dressed and opened the door a crack. Captain Austin stood with a lantern in one hand and a bedraggled boy in the other. Behind them both was the black man named Apollo who had rowed her in the scow. He stood a respectful distance holding something awkwardly in his hands.

"Ma'am, please excuse the interruption," Captain Austin said politely. "I am wondering if you recognize this fellow. Claims to be a servant. Keeps saying your name. Your whole name. We don't ordinarily allow deck passengers up here in cabin class. But I thought just in case he might be lost property." He winked. "You know what I mean."

Rosita pulled the shawl tightly around herself. She squinted in the sudden, bright light. The shivering boy tried to wriggle free, but Captain Austin held him tight and lowered the lantern next to the boy's muddy face.

María! Rosita clenched her teeth. *Ruining everything again.*

"Rosita!" María squeaked.

"Doesn't know his place very well, does he?" Captain Austin gave the irritating deckhand a quick shake. "Is he one of your slaves?"

Rosita frowned. "Slavery is not allowed in Mexico, *señor.*"

Captain Austin grinned broadly at her. "Oh, you go along now! I suppose I'm just green from the States. I don't know all the customs around here yet."

Green from the states? Rosita was puzzled by his words and amused glance. *What does he mean by 'go along now'?*

"Texas may be part of Mexico—at least for the moment," Captain Austin said smugly. "Where I come from a right smart man has ways to get around such nit-picking Mexican laws, *señorita.*"

Rosita bristled. She was uncertain if he were making fun of her or her country. Since she had no money to pay for her fare, she decided she could not risk confronting this *norteamericano*. In Guerrero she had often heard her father and his friends talk about *los primos*, these so-called "cousins" from Texas who had been given land north of the Río Bravo by the Mexican government. The Texans had promised that they would worship in Catholic churches, not bring slaves into their country, and obey the Mexican government, which had been newly freed from Spanish rule.

"And what about this?" Captain Austin nudged Apollo, who held out a book. "We found this among his possessions. Must have stolen it. It's got a woman's name inside, see?"

Rosita looked at the book of poetry, which she recognized immediately as her stepsister's prized possession. How perfectly stupid of María to bring something like a book along with her! Everyone knew that servants couldn't read.

"Well, what should we do with the fellow?" Captain Austin wondered aloud as he held the lantern aloft. "Throw him overboard for theft? Might make a nice dinner for some big river catfish."

"No, *señor*. That won't be necessary. You see, the book is mine. It belonged to my . . . mother. My servant was delivering the book when we were . . . we were separated on our way to your steamboat. I'm so glad you found him *and* the book," Rosita said quickly. She knew María was trembling, but she refused to look at her. *She deserves to be left ashore but then what will happen to me? She'll run back to town and tell everyone where I am.* "I will pay extra for the servant's passage," she added, unsure of how she would even manage to pay her own fare.

Captain Austin gave a pleased chuckle. He had lost a deckhand but gained a paying passenger.

"*Señor?*" María said politely. "I tried to warn you."

"Warn us of what?" Captain Austin replied. He released his grip on María's collar.

"Warn you of what I saw on shore. Bandits armed and waiting to attack your ship. I heard them before I came on board. With my own ears."

"The bandits who attacked?" Captain Austin said. "Why did no one tell me?"

"*Señor*, I tried to tell your man with the big voice. He did not listen. He told me to carry wood."

"McCallister, the ship's mate?"

María nodded.

Captain Austin took a deep breath. "I will speak to him. Sometimes his judgment is faulty. Knowing there were bandits about to ambush could have saved us a lot of trouble. We might have been prepared."

"I will personally vouch for this . . . this boy's honesty," said Rosita, who had never once heard María lie. She looked at her stepsister with a narrow gaze that could mean only one thing. *Keep your mouth shut about who I am and I will keep my mouth shut about who you are.*

"Fine, fine," Captain Austin said distractedly. He turned to Apollo and gave him orders in English. Apollo hurried away. *"Señorita,"* he said politely to Rosita, "good night."

"Buenas noches," Rosita said. She gripped María's arm tightly and steered her back inside the cabin. When they were both inside and the door was shut behind them, Rosita turned to her stepsister and hissed angrily, "What are you doing here?"

"I am going to the ocean, too," María insisted.

"Keep your voice down. Was that true what you told Austin?"

María nodded. She glanced around the room. It was much more magnificent than anything she had experienced below deck.

Rosita examined her stepsister curiously. She could hardly believe anyone as timid as María would cut her hair, put on boy's clothes, slip out of the house alone, make her way past bandits, and convince the wooding party to take her aboard ship. What had gotten into her? "Did anyone from the village see you in your ridiculous disguise?"

María shook her head, then told Rosita what had happened in Guerrero since she vanished.

"Frida, the liar!" Rosita exclaimed.

"She is a colorful storyteller, is she not?" María said, trying to keep from laughing. "Now the whole village is terrified of you. It reminds me of a song."

"Sing it," Rosita said, pleased to have been made so famous.

And María sang all the verses to *"La ciudad de Jauja"* about an adventurer who went to a fantastic land where the churches were made of sugar and ducks flew about already seasoned with salt and pepper. Trees grew tortillas, the fields sprouted crops of turnovers, and the streets were lined with *tamales turcos.*

> *"¿Qué dices, amigo? vamos*
> *a ver si dicen verdad,*
> *si es verdad lo que dicen*
> *nos quedaremos allá."*

> (What do you say, friend? Let us go
> see if they're speaking the truth;
> if all they say is true,
> we will remain there.)

As María sang, the passengers in cabin class stopped what they were doing to listen. *"Señorita?"* Madame de la Barca said, knocking on Rosita's door. "Is it you with the lovely voice? Come out and sing for us."

Rosita opened the door, surprised by all the people staring at her. "It is not me. It is my servant."

"Then have your servant sing."

María seemed too embarrassed to sing in front of so many strangers. "I will play my violin to accompany you," Rosita promised. "Then it will not seem so frightening."

María reluctantly agreed. They stepped outside into the saloon and performed a duet. The passengers applauded. "More, please, more," Madame de la Barca said. The passengers seemed to enjoy the entertainment so much, they did not want them to stop. María sang all kinds of songs. Rosita, who was not an accomplished musician, simply played a few notes to accompany her. María led the performance, smiling radiantly. Her voice soared over the river. When it was very late and they had no more energy to perform, Rosita excused herself and her servant and retreated to her cabin.

"No one told me to sing softer," María said happily. She glanced at the pillow and yawned.

"If you think you're sleeping on one of the bunks, you are mistaken," Rosita said. "You are the servant, remember? You sleep outside on the saloon floor."

María gathered a blanket and a pillow stuffed with corncobs to make a bed on the floor. Before she left, Rosita turned to her and said, "When we get to Matamoros, we shall go our separate ways. Is that understood?"

"Certainly."

Rosita opened the door and held a candle so that María could see to make her bed on the saloon floor. Compared to the place she'd slept the night before, the saloon rug seemed quite luxurious to María. "Now go to sleep," Rosita commanded.

"Is Matamoros near the ocean?"

Rosita sighed. "Matamoros is as far as this boat travels."

"You must call me José," María whispered. "That is my name."

"*Buenas noches, José,*" Rosita said. She tried to sound impatient, but somehow she couldn't help grinning.

"*Buenas noches, señorita,*" María replied as Rosita blew out the candle.

Chapter

8

The next morning as the *Ariel* chugged downstream, Rosita leaned on the balcony railing and
gazed out over the moving water from the cabin-
deck promenade. María sat nearby, dozing in the
shade. *She's missing everything,* Rosita thought. She
glanced at her stepsister with a kind of grudging
admiration, recalling their triumph performing for
the other passengers.

Sometimes wide, sometimes narrow, the river
churned and shouldered against midstream islands
and rocks and the fallen debris from powerful
floods and rains of seasons past. Seagulls swooped
overhead. Turtles sunned themselves along the
muddy shore that was lined with snag heaps. Herds
of timid antelope waded in the shallows. Flocks of

ducks glided silently through the loose, racing waters. Gullies harbored hidden, serenading bull-frogs and lightning-white birds. For a split second at a time Rosita spied secret pools cradling dead leaves and branches webbed with muck.

A deer lapping water at the edge of the river looked up with enormous eyes at the hissing boat. The paddle wheels chopped along sweetly, dripping water on a clear run. For a few yards there were no twists or turns, no tortuous bends or loops.

"AHEEEEE!" the steam whistle shrieked and let off a plume of white steam.

The deer bounded away.

While Rosita was admiring the scenery, high in the pilothouse Rackliffe stood at the wheel and scanned the river ahead for ripples and rapids and narrows. His pale blue eyes moved back and forth reading the color and the texture of the water that might warn of perilous bars of sand or gravel or — worse yet — rock. He searched for clues revealing underwater snags — driftwood and sawyers, whole trees buried like sharp pikes waiting to tear the hull out of the boat. He could not relax his attention for even thirty seconds. Although he had piloted this stretch of river upstream, the downstream route now revealed a whole new river. The Río Grande changed constantly, shifting as the water level dropped dangerously lower and lower. Every delay meant that they were that much more likely to be trapped — that their enterprise would fail.

He rang a bell, the signal to the engineer below on the main deck. The boat slowed.

"Wood-pile! Wood-pile!" someone shouted on the main deck.

María's eyes opened. She stretched and slowly joined Rosita at the railing.

"Why are we stopping?" Rosita asked.

"Fuel." María winced recalling the pain in her back from hauling wood from shore. "The crew goes ashore to chop whatever they can find for the boiler."

"The boiler?" Rosita asked. She did not know this word.

Suddenly they heard brisk footsteps approach. *"Buenos días, señorita,"* Captain Austin said. He smiled pleasantly and tipped his hat.

"The boiler, *señor,"* Rosita asked in a sweet voice. "What is this?"

"The boiler heats water that powers this boat," Captain Austin explained. "Steam pushes through the pipes and makes these paddle wheels on each side of the ship move. Without wood, no fire. Without fire, no steam. Without steam, we're stuck here like a pig in a poke. That's why when we send the wooding parties ashore, we keep the cannons pointed on the bluffs and rifles ready in case of snipers from shore. They keep a sharp lookout for more *banditos* or Comanche. We suspect that Indians have been following us on shore for the last five miles."

"How do you know?" Rosita asked nervously.

"Certain signs, certain signals they give each other. They are clever and move almost silently on horseback."

Rosita looked down and spotted two deckhands with guns. She wondered if there were Indians watching them right at this very moment.

"I trust you are enjoying your voyage, *señorita,*" Captain Austin said to Rosita. "I notice that you are not wearing your fine jewelry today."

"No, *señor,*" Rosita said nervously. The way he smiled at her made her skin crawl. She was glad she had hidden the necklace.

"I'd like to take up the subject of the fare for you and your servant. Mr. Oliver tells me you still have not paid."

Rosita's heart beat faster and faster.

"I've purposefully put you in the cabin farthest from the boiler," he continued.

"Muchas gracias," she replied, trying to keep her voice calm, steady. She glanced at María, who seemed equally disturbed.

"Don't thank me. I did it for my own protection."

Captain Austin's voice had an unpleasant edge to it. "That cabin's the safest in case of an explosion. And seeing that you haven't paid, well, let's just say I'm hedging my bets."

Rosita gulped.

"Now, *señorita*, I've been patient. But enough is enough. You look like a fine, well-off lady. I need your money this morning."

"*Sí, señor*. I will pay you," Rosita said sweetly. "*Mañana*."

Captain Austin's face began to turn quite red. "No, not *mañana*. Right now."

"But *señor*—"

"No more excuses, *señorita*. Your fare must be paid or you and your servant will be put ashore."

Now she had no choice. "If you will wait here, *señor*, I will fetch something. Something valuable." She went inside the cabin.

María followed her and stood outside the cabin doorway. "Not the necklace," she hissed. She knew how much it meant to her stepsister.

"What choice do I have?" Rosita replied angrily. But when she lifted the corner of the mattress, there was nothing there. Rosita felt too stunned to move, to speak.

"What's wrong?" María squeaked.

"It's gone!"

Frantically, they searched for the necklace inside the blanket, under the pillow, on the floor. They pulled the mattress from the bed and shook it. And they did this all again a second time, then a third, growing more and more desperate.

"*Señorita?*" Captain Austin called impatiently.

"One moment," Rosita replied. Her enormous eyes filled with terror. They would be put ashore among the Indians, the bandits. Her mother's precious necklace had been stolen right from under her own eyes. She would never see it again. How could this have happened? "*Señor*, I wish to report a theft," she said in a trembling voice.

"Do not trifle with me, *señorita*. Where is the necklace?" Captain Austin demanded.

"Stolen," Rosita murmured.

"Well, a stolen necklace is of little use to me," Captain Austin replied. "That is not my problem. Do you have cash?"

Rosita shook her head. "Perhaps I might offer you a fine violin?"

María watched her stepsister anxiously. The sacrifice of the violin? She tried to signal silently to Rosita to stop. There had to be some other way to pay their fare. She recalled how she had worked on the wooding crew and was allowed on board. Suddenly she felt inspired.

"I do not have any use for a musical instrument," Captain Austin replied in a cold voice. "I'm afraid—"

"*Señor?*" María interrupted. "I have heard that your cook quit."

"Who told you?" Captain Austin looked at Rosita's servant with alarm. News traveled fast. The cook had run off just the night before. These servants—always talking. How was he ever going to keep the cabin passengers satisfied now? They were ready to lynch him. Now this—

"My mistress is a fine cook," María continued. "Perhaps she can cook for you. I could help her. We could pay our fare by working in your kitchen."

Rosita looked at María in surprise. What was she saying? Neither of them had ever cooked for so many people before.

"I do need a cook." Captain Austin scratched his head as if he were considering the impertinent servant's idea. "All right," he said gruffly. "You'll have to move below."

"Below?" Rosita said in a small, confused voice.

"You don't think you'll take up my best cabin if you're cooking, do you? If you're part of the crew, you sleep below. I suggest you get your belongings together and move quickly before I change my mind. You report to McCallister now." Captain Austin marched away.

*　　*　　*

Unlike María, who had already tasted what life was like below deck, Rosita was quite shocked to discover that instead of a bed she would have to sleep on the floor. She would have none of the comforts or conveniences of the cabin passengers. On deck she soon discovered there was no saloon, no fancy glass, no plush, no gilt, no glitter—however faded. Rosita and María found a bale to sleep on. They discovered that a communal bucket was all that was available to scoop water from the river to wash with. There was no private water closet.

"Make way! Make way!" McCallister shouted and cursed in English. He knocked a few deck passengers aside to pull through a long rope. When he saw Rosita he paused and gave her a long, nasty look. "Glad to see you down here with the rest of us deckers. Not so fancy now, are you, Miss High and Mighty?"

"*¡Arriban los corazones!*" María whispered to Rosita to give her courage. She could not understand the mate's words—only their cruel intent.

María gave her stepsister a look of warning to be still and give no offense.

Rosita curtsied and replied to McCallister in an ingratiating voice, "*Sí señor puerco.*"

Fortunately McCallister spoke little Spanish and

did not realize what she had just called him. He smiled, looped the rope over his shoulder, and disappeared.

"Rosita, do not call him a pig!" María hissed, terrified. She had seen what had happened to Carlos when he offended the all-powerful mate. His eye was still black and blue. "That was a very dangerous thing to do. You must be as invisible and obedient as possible in McCallister's presence. If you make him angry, he might throw us off the ship."

Rosita simply clucked. "I am not afraid of him."

"You should be. He is your boss," María replied. "Now come. I will show you the kitchen, the place they call the galley."

Rosita and her stepsister walked around boxes and bales and sleeping bodies, families lounging in the shade and then climbed the stairs to the cabin area and crossed the saloon to the galley, which was located amidship near the wheelhouse. The galley was so small, it was difficult for even one person to fit inside. A filthy wood-burning stove, cast iron and black with grease, sat against one smoke-stained wall. There was a small table directly opposite. On the walls hung blackened pots and pans and an assortment of spoons still caked in places with crusty bits of food. On the floor stood a pail of scummy water. It seemed clear that the former cook had left the kitchen in the midst of cooking.

"What's in here?" María asked. She opened the top of a barrel containing a few pounds of rice that crawled with black bugs. In another barrel were dried peas and in another cornmeal. The cornmeal wiggled suspiciously with maggots, small white worms. A stone jar contained a few pounds of rancid-smelling salt pork; another held salt beef, which was called "salt horse" by the deckhands. A tin, when pried open, revealed assorted hard, dried square hardtack crackers crawling with weevils. Rat droppings littered the floor.

Now Rosita understood why the saloon table featured almost exclusively wild game. There was hardly anything else edible on board. "How shall we make a decent meal from what's here?" Rosita complained. In her father's house the kitchen was well stocked, clean, and furnished with the best copper pans and proper utensils. There were servants to clean up after the cook. Here they would not only have to do their own cooking, but they would also have to wash the pans and dishes.

María sighed. "Not promising."

"No wonder the cook ran away." Rosita gingerly picked up a sour-smelling rag between two fingers.

"Well, there's nothing else to be done. We must

get to work," María said. She tied a piece of burlap sack around her waist and picked up a bucket. "I'll dump this and get some fresh water. We'll begin by cleaning."

Reluctantly, Rosita did as she was told. The task seemed impossible. For the next several hours, she and her stepsister scrubbed and cleaned the pots and pans, the blackened stove. They washed the table with great vigor. As they worked, María sang.

Carlos stoked the cooking stove with fresh wood. "Here is the meat for supper," he said and winked. He dumped eight scrawny chickens on the floor. While María plucked and cleaned the chickens, Rosita found a sad, old onion. She chopped this up. When the fat was sizzling in a large pot, she threw the onion in and cooked it. "It is too bad we have no spices," Rosita said. The chickens were cut up into pieces and added to the pot to cook.

There was no *metate*, a three-legged stone with a long roller for grinding corn. There was no *comal* on which to fry the tortillas. "It is too bad we cannot soak and grind the corn the proper way. Tortillas taste better when they are ground fresh on the *metate*," María complained. "They taste better cooked on a proper *comal.*"

"Can't be helped." Rosita examined the barrel containing the cornmeal. The *masa harina* was made from parched corn kernels that had been soaked in a solution of unslaked lime and water before they were ground. She gulped and shook the maggots from the coarse cornmeal using a rusty sieve.

María pointed to the wriggling bugs. "Here are your spices," she said with a perfectly straight face.

"Very funny," Rosita replied.

María measured several handfuls of *masa harina* into a tin bowl. She added just enough water and mixed the dough quickly and lightly. Together María and Rosita scooped out fistfuls of dough. They patted the sticky dough in a familiar kitchen rhythm that made them both suddenly feel homesick. Back and forth, back and forth, from one hand to the other, they patted the dough into a thin round pancake shape.

It was difficult for them not to think of the delicious turnovers of corn dough filled with cheese, potatoes, and squash flowers. They could not help imagining the spicy meat wrapped in tortillas, so well seasoned and fragrant with chile and tomatoes. The brown and black and green *moles*, delicious sauces that doña Álvarez knew how to make so skillfully.

Rosita set the heavy iron skillet on the stove with a small amount of fat. When the fat sizzled, María placed the first tortilla in the greased skillet. As soon as the tortilla began to dry out around the edges, she flipped it over and cooked it for a slightly longer time on the second side, the way her mother had taught her.

"Now it begins to color," María told Rosita. María flipped it over again to the first side so that the tortilla could cook through. She watched with pleasure as the tortilla's plump little face began to puff up invitingly in the center. She slipped the tortilla from the pan on to a plate, covered it with a cloth, and began the next one. Soon there was a great stack of tortillas ready.

Rosita made an enormous fresh pot of coffee. Although there was little else to eat stored on board, there was plenty of coffee. When the food was ready, María carried in the dishes and placed them on the long table for the cabin passengers. Rosita watched anxiously from the stifling galley as the group assembled, taking their seats around the table.

Suddenly Rosita had a terrible thought. "What if they hate the food?" she whispered to María.

"Too late now," María replied.

Chapter 9

"A great improvement over burned pork, beans hard as rock, and charred corn bread," Captain Austin announced. He winked at Rosita and her steward. Rosita breathed a great sigh of relief.

The other passengers ate furiously, too busy to do anything more than grunt their approval. "We could use more meat, sir," Madame de la Barca announced. "This is hardly enough for the company present."

"Never fear, ma'am," Captain Austin said. "We will be stopping soon at Mier and our stores will be replenished. In the meantime I will send hunters ashore for fresh game."

After the guests left the table, there was little left to serve to the hungry crew. María made more tortillas and fried another scrawny chicken. Carlos showed Rosita and María a bag of potatoes hidden especially for the crew. These potatoes were boiled and hastily combined with whatever was left from the saloon table—grizzled chicken, fresh tortillas— and scraped haphazardly into large pans.

"Grub-pile! Grub-pile!" Carlos shouted and carried the pans below. The roustabouts and other deckhands, McCallister included, took their seats on the open deck and clawed into the various flat iron pans to get hold of whatever pieces of meat or potato they could. Some used their hands. Others scooped the food on to pieces of hardtack, which they used as a kind of plate.

"Not an appetizing spectacle," Rosita murmured. María nodded. She felt as if she might be sick.

When Rosita and María returned to the galley, they began the backbreaking job of cleaning the pans and washing the dishes that had been scattered helter-skelter all over the saloon table. They dipped the greasy dishes in large tubs of sudsy river water and wiped them with seed sack scraps. When they finished, they had hardly enough time to catch their breath before they had to begin fixing the next meal.

This was the hardest Rosita had ever worked in her life. It amazed her to think that all these years in her father's house she had never stopped to consider the servants who had labored tirelessly to provide her with food. María did not mind the work. Time flew because she was working alongside her stepsister, who ordinarily avoided or ignored her.

"I think we did very well," María said cheerfully.

"I am glad you have such a gratifying sense of accomplishment," Rosita replied wearily. "As for myself, I think that I could sleep for a year."

Rosita leaned out over the deck and fanned herself with her makeshift apron. The shoreline rumbled past. Water splashed gently against the sides of the ship. María joined her at the railing, contentedly nibbling a tortilla. And for the first time in ever so long, she felt hopeful that everything would work out after all.

The next day's cooking proceeded more smoothly. The hunting party succeeded in bringing back a variety of meat, including squirrel, pigeon, several wild ducks, and a large wild turkey. Rosita had begged the hunters to bring back some leaves of the *nopal*, the prickly-pear cactus and perhaps a few of the fruits, called *tunas*, if they were available. She had visions of cooking these with chile. But since no chile was available anywhere on the boat and since the hunters hurt their hands and did not know how to safely remove the spiky cactus leaves, there would be no delicious *nopal*.

Rosita felt a little like a failure as a cook. But for some strange reason, the cabin passengers did not notice her deficiencies. The former cook was so terrible, so filthy, so drunk and uninspired, that whatever Rosita and her new steward provided seemed a welcome change. The new fare actually seemed to improve shipboard morale.

"Nicely done, *señorita*," Oliver said, and tipped his hat one afternoon after supper.

This pleased Rosita enormously. As for María, she found the work in the kitchen much safer and less arduous than working on the wooding crew. While the meals were cooking, she had a chance to sit and look out at the river.

Once María thought she spied a lonely shepherd staring down from the flood-cut banks. The figure quickly vanished in terror. María smiled. She was not afraid. She knew what the ship was about and it no longer scared her. Riding along gave her a sense of accomplishment, of power—something she had never had before. She was more than just a terrified spectator or even a passenger. She was an important member of the crew. She helped cook the food.

This was the farthest she had ever traveled from

home in her life. Everything seemed new and exciting. "Ah, come and look!" she called to Rosita one afternoon. A herd of wild horses galloped across the plains of mesquite on the other side of the river. Dust rolled and hung in the hot air.

Rosita sighed. "The wood pile near the engine room grows smaller and smaller and Austin grows more and more impatient."

"We can certainly drift along on the current, can't we?" María asked hopefully.

"To steer a ship of this size he says he must have fuel to move the great paddle wheels," Rosita said. "Have you not seen how Austin paces and frets? 'Not fast enough,' he says. 'Not fast enough. Time is money.' What does that mean?"

María shrugged. "These *norteamericanos* have curious ways."

The next day the heat grew intense. There seemed no where to hide to escape the bright light. One by one the pigs corralled into small pens began to die. The smell was intolerable. Rosita refused to cook the meat from the dead animals for fear they might be sickened, too. This disturbed Austin, who angrily ordered Apollo to pitch the bloated carcasses overboard.

That night the mosquitoes attacked in hungry clouds. Even the bright torches that swung out from poles on the deck and the smoky smudge pots burning on deck could not keep away the stinging, hungry hordes. When morning came the faces of Rosita and her stepsister were swollen with bites. As the heat increased, the water level of the river dropped dangerously lower and lower. Worse yet, game disappeared.

When Rosita and María served a meal of tough salt horse, the crew grumbled. They no longer joked or sang. McCallister stared glumly at the bluffs, his rifle close by. No one spoke.

"What's wrong?" Rosita whispered.

"Comanche," María said and scooped up some beans with a stale tortilla. She tilted her head. "They've been following us."

Rosita looked out over the bluffs but she could see nothing. If the ship came too close to shore, it would be easy enough for ambushers to shoot down at them. Nervously, she scooted toward the middle of the deck, where she rolled and slapped fresh tortilla dough. Back and forth between her hands she threw the tortillas. *Smack. Smack-smack-smack.* "Help me now. You said you would, lazy one."

"What is this?" María demanded. She pointed to a piece of canvas covering a large metal object that jutted in strange directions like elbows of a constrained giant. She peeked curiously under the canvas.

"Do not touch that," Rosita advised.

"What harm is there in one quick peek?" María replied. She crawled beneath the canvas for a better look.

"Out, pest!" barked Captain Austin. "Do not meddle with my printing press."

"Sorry, *señor*," María said shamefacedly. She backed out from under the canvas and bowed, careful to keep her gaze on her bare feet. "I was only curious what it is. What it does."

"A printing press makes books, newspapers — anything you like," Captain Austin replied. He hooked his thumbs in his suspenders. "By writing about the wonders, the resources along the river, I hope to induce civilized people to immigrate here."

María looked puzzled. "How would a printing press do that?"

"By letting people know what is here. What is possible. If only I could find enough paper."

"Ah, *sí, señor*," María replied with growing enthusiasm. "Books. Newspapers. A wonderful idea."

Captain Austin scratched his head and looked at her curiously. "I have met few Mexicans who can read. Especially among servants."

"Don't pay any attention to this one, *señor*,"

Rosita interrupted. She gave her stepsister a look of warning. "This servant has a big mouth full of great boasts and dreams."

"Ambition is nothing to be ashamed of," Austin said. Carefully, he retied a rope to secure the canvas around the printing press. "At the age of twelve I sailed to China as a cabin boy. When I returned I discovered that my father had died and left me responsible for my family. I quit the sea and went to work in New York. I, too, was filled with ambition in those days." He leaned against the wall and lit a foul-smelling cigar.

"You must be a very lucky man to have acquired enough money to buy this marvelous boat," Rosita said, hoping to disarm him with flattery so that he might forget María's blunder.

Austin blew a smoke ring and laughed harshly. "Scarce a dollar that has gone out of my hands has returned to me. This venture is my last chance. I've left my wife and daughters home in the East. Dear things, I scarcely remember what they look like. I hope to retrieve my ruined fortune and lay a foundation for an estate for my family by securing a large tract of land.

"Think of it. Just five years ago I came to Texas upon the urging of my cousin, who wrote to me long, fascinating letters. I tried to set up a gin and commission business in Mexico. This failed. Then I bought the *Ariel* to navigate three hundred miles up the river. I have had a long life of incessant enterprise, toil, privation, and suffering. But I will not give up. Not yet."

Throughout this long speech, Rosita marveled at the white man's monkey speech in Spanish. His tick-tack ways. His fascination with money and fortune. The incessant tick-tack of work and toil and suffering. How he went on and on about yesterday, tomorrow, and today—this exactitude of time. And even as he spoke he kept ordering the other crew members about, forever mechanically bossing them all in circles. No wonder he could not understand the Mexican idea of *mañana*. No wonder he could not understand that the only real times were the fixed points of birth, death, and fiestas. That was all there was.

Rosita sighed. She listened as if interested but her mind wandered. Captain Austin seemed a tortured soul. A man who was far from home and restless. His ways were not her ways. She could not understand him. In spite of his gentlemanly habits and gracious attitude, she found she could not trust him. He never helped her try to find who stole her necklace. She suspected it was the cook or possibly the gambler, both of whom disappeared. To her,

Captain Austin was simply someone to use to get to the place she wanted to go. That was all.

Suddenly a cry went up from the pilothouse. A bell rang. Rosita dropped the tortilla she was patting into shape. María staggered forward. Captain Austin cursed in English and hurried away. For several moments all was confusion. Apollo ran to the ship's side and looked out over the water.

"What happened?" María demanded.

Water sloshed and foamed as the paddle wheels rotated backward in the water. "Maybe we're stuck," Rosita said. Then she grabbed her sister by the arm and turned her so that she could stare into her face. "Next time, do not answer so truthfully to the captain. You nearly ruined your disguise just now."

"What do you mean?"

"Servants are not taught to read. You know that," Rosita whispered. "Your grandfather's remarkably odd idea of teaching you to read books has not helped your brain one bit, foolish one. Can't you remember who you're pretending to be? A servant. Remember. You are a servant."

Sheepishly, María shrugged. "Sorry," she said in a soft voice. "If I had enough money I would buy that printing press myself."

"What would you do with such a thing?" Rosita demanded.

"I would print books. I would print songs and poems."

Rosita rolled her eyes. What foolish talk! Her stepsister was *loca*.

The paddle wheels thrashed in the opposite direction. *Ariel* rocked and pulled away from the sandbar it had landed on. Austin, clearly anxious to escape, kept a close eye on the steep bluffs on either side of the river. He glanced every now and again through a telescope.

When they reached a bend in the river, Apollo was ordered to row ashore to chop whatever wood he could find. Carlos and a few other deckhands joined him while McCallister kept watch with a rifle in case any Comanche appeared. They slapped themselves over and over as they were quickly enveloped in a cloud of mosquitoes.

Rosita filled a tub with brown river water and washed a pan with a rag. She handed each dish to María, who kept her eyes on the bluffs, watching for any sign of movement. Except for the sound of mosquitoes buzzing, the river was quiet.

Too quiet.

Chapter

10

In the distance Rosita and her stepsister listened for the sound of axes biting wood. For the sounds of gunfire. They scarcely breathed as they dipped each tin plate into the water and rubbed it dry.

"Will they hurry?" María whispered.

The sun began to dip on the horizon. Finally, after what seemed like endless waiting, the wood choppers rowed back to the ship with their load of spindly branches, a few logs of ebony and willow.

A shot rang out just as Apollo pulled himself exhausted and sweating on to the boat. Rosita and María dove for cover behind a barrel of molasses. McCallister shouted orders. He fired back.

Sparks sprang from the chimney. The boat lurched forward into racing waters. For once their luck held. They managed to escape safely around a fist of islands and reefs that stood up like knuckles in the current. And the band of Comanche on shore was left far behind.

That evening the steamboat anchored in a safe place in the middle of the river. Some of the crew gathered on boxes and bales on the main deck where the lanterns were lit. A few passengers lingered around the edges of the group. Apollo made everyone laugh when he imitated the great monster that had once owned a giant bone he found at the river's edge. He lumbered about the deck with the fearsome stomping of the enormous beast. The leg bone itself was a kind of marvel. Standing on end it came nearly to Rosita's shoulder.

In honor of Apollo's find and the sudden sense of safety that their escape gave them, María and Rosita played a duet. For once the deckhands seemed to relax in the torchlight. It felt good to be alive — even though they were bitten by mosquitoes and hungrier than they liked. They had wood to power their ship. They had evaded their enemies.

Rackliffe announced a card game. "Poker," he said and winked at Rosita. He snapped a grubby deck of cards that he took from his back pocket on the table. The crew members gathered around.

Rosita blushed and quickly ushered María away

from the place the men were playing. "It is not proper," she hissed protectively in the ear of her stepsister, who wanted very much to learn how to play.

Rackliffe quickly won the meager earnings from the two deckhands. Apollo had no money. He didn't play. Instead, he watched, keeping a wary eye on the pistol in Rackliffe's holster. With a gun and some knowledge of Spanish he might escape and vanish into the backcountry where nobody would ever find him. Slavery in Mexico was illegal now. Captain Austin and the others passed him off as an indentured servant. But the truth remained that he was Austin's slave.

María sat beside Apollo and offered him some of the salve to soothe mosquito bites that Rosita had prepared from the aloe of a cactus. He took the salve and seemed to understand when she pretended to rub it on her own hand. *"Mano,"* she said.

"Mano," he repeated, holding up his hand. Then he pointed to his eye.

She smiled. *"Ojo."* She pointed to her nose. *"Nariz."*

He repeated each word she said in Spanish and tried in turn to teach her the English equivalent. She enjoyed helping him understand Spanish. It made her feel very important to show a grownup how to speak her language.

He stuck out one big, bare foot.

"Pie," she replied.

He had no way to tell her that if he could get far enough away, fast enough on foot into the back-country, he'd be free. Captain Austin would never follow him. Apollo knew how to be patient. He would wait and watch, and when the time was right, he would disappear.

Early the next morning the river offered its first straight, deep channel. Today was the big day—the day the boat would make time, Captain Austin announced. The deckhands hurried to prepare for the event that the bored cabin passengers had long awaited—to feel the steamboat move. To experience just how fast the *Ariel* could go.

"Take a tray of food down to the boiler room for the engineer," Rosita told her sister. "They say we're firing up for a fast run. We've got to move before this river goes any lower."

"Sí," María said. She had never been inside the boiler room and the idea terrified her. Carlos had described Ira Belknap, the engineer, as some kind of hideous *monstruo*. But she had to go. She was a servant. She had to do as she was told.

"Señor?" she squeaked at the main deck. She nearly dropped the tray of food when Belknap

turned and looked at her. One side of his face was purplish and disfigured like a rotten piece of fruit. The hair on one side of his head was mostly gone and his scalp looked brittle and pink. His scars were the result of a terrible steamboat explosion four years earlier. He cocked his head and looked at her with his one good eye, motioning for her to bring the food inside the rumbling boiler room.

Belknap's job was essential but invisible. He kept the tottering old boiler going, coaxing one more day of life out of the overused machinery. He was a shadowy presence rarely seen by the other deck passengers, even though the great roaring furnace occupied the center of the boat's main deck. The furnace had just been stoked with wood and roared loudly.

María cowered in the doorway. The great gaping door of the furnace was closed. Belknap had just finished cleaning out river mud from the boiler for the second time that day. His shirt was black with mire and grease; his neck and arms glistened with sweat. He balanced on a stool and tinkered with a leaking joint on one of the boiler's many cracked and bandaged pipes. "What do you want, boy?" Belknap demanded in English.

"*Por favor,*" she said quietly. She put the tray on the floor and tried not to breathe his odor, which reminded her of decaying pumpkin. He did not even look at her. "*Señor* Austin —"

"That fool intends to blow us all sky high," Belknap said angrily. "Wants me to shove this boiler faster than she's intended. I'll tell you, it's the engineer that gets killed first when the whole thing explodes. Always the engineer."

"*Sí, señor,*" María answered. She did not understand a word of what he was telling her but she stood there politely and listened all the same. The roaring machinery fascinated her. She had never seen anything so enormous and terrible in her life. The man's strange manner enthralled her, too. She wondered if this was what the visiting priest had meant when he described the devil.

Belknap grabbed a piece of meat and chewed it as he examined a blown-out cylinder head. "Talk about northern steamers. It don't need any spunk to navigate them waters. Sure, I bet you've never seen a boiler bust. I tell you, boy, it takes a man to ride one of them half alligator boats, head on a snag, high pressure, safety valve soldered down, two hundred souls on board and all in danger of losing their lives."

"*Sí, señor,*" María said. She jumped when she heard the bells hanging overhead mysteriously begin to clang all by themselves.

"Ah, yes, Rackliffe!" Belknap hollered at the clanging bell. "I hear you. I hear you." Quick as a cat, Belknap began making adjustments here and there, rotating wheels and pressing levers to control the boiler according to the bell signals he received from Rackliffe high in the pilothouse. Belknap tilted his head to one side and listened to the roar of steam in the great boiler that told him that pressure set had been reached. The bells began a crazy chorus, sometimes ringing once, then twice.

"Listen to that feller, would you? First he says, 'Stop.' Then, 'Go back.' Then, 'Come ahead again.' Then, 'Slow.' Then, 'Come ahead full steam.' Then, 'Stop.' Thinks he's a real hot, close-fit pilot. Twenty years old. He's just a pup." Belknap shook his head. "He'll get us all killed yet."

"*Sí, señor,*" María said. The boat was beginning to roar and tremble so loudly she could hardly hear him. The plate on the tray rattled uncontrollably. She staggered backward. Her feet, her arms, her teeth seemed to be vibrating from the power that raced from the boiler. Could such an evil machine give her *mal ojo* or some other curse?

Terrified, she ran out of the boiler room. Just as she reached the stairway and was starting up, several passengers climbed down and knocked her aside. They were shouting and laughing and pointing to the scenery speeding past. Wind blew their hair and they seemed excited and exhilarated as they shouted up to the pilothouse, "Faster! Faster!"

María hurried to the galley, convinced that something terrible was going to happen any moment. She had seen the devil down in the belly of the ship. She had seen him with her own eyes.

"What is it?" Rosita said. She stood in the galley doorway with a plucked duck.

"Rosita—"

Crash! María was knocked to the floor. Her stepsister flew past out the door of the galley. A saloon mirror fell from the wall. Chairs skidded. Plates shattered. There was a terrible grinding noise. And then a thundering moment of complete silence. The engine had stopped. The motionless paddle wheels dripped.

"Rosita?" María squeaked. She could hear cries and screams.

"María, are you all right?" Rosita asked in a hoarse voice. She sprawled on the saloon floor, still clutching a half-plucked duck.

"I am all right. Nothing broken," María said slowly from the place where she had tumbled on to the floor of the saloon. She moved her arms, her legs.

McCallister dashed past swearing and kicking

away the debris. He was followed by two other deckhands, including Apollo.

"Another sandbar?" María asked in a dazed voice.

"Of course. What else could it be?" Rosita replied. She stood slowly and looked around her. Two legs were sticking out of the clerk's office. She recognized the large, wide boots immediately. "*Señor* Oliver!" she called. "Help me, María."

Together the girls began to try to unearth the buried clerk from a mound of paper and books and receipts and broken plates caked with dried food. Carefully, Rosita said a few words and waved a book in front of his face to give him some air. Oliver seemed to be breathing. He sat up, but his eyes were vacant and confused. His hair stood straight up in wild tufts.

From below came the grinding of the capstan, the cries of the deckhands, the shouts of commands. McCallister cursed loudly. Bells signaled. The boat creaked and shook.

"*Señor?*" Rosita said. She gently patted Oliver's fat cheeks. She wished she had some *poleo*, the herb her mother used when people suffered from fright sickness. She could make some tea. "Speak to me, *señor*. Are you all right? Can you speak?"

Oliver turned and looked at her and began talking in fluent Spanish. "Mother, I have told you before. The drug store business is plodding and slow. Steamboating is the very opposite of this. Every trip is a venture, Mother. There's constant hurry and confusion and change of scenery and constant anxiety about the success of the enterprise. Failure, profit—they're always possible, always probable."

"What's wrong with him?" María whispered. "He thinks you're his mother."

Rosita bit her lip. "Perhaps he hit his head."

"The very adventurous nature of the business has a charm for me, Mother," Oliver continued. "I feel as if nothing could ever induce me to return to the dull confinement of the drug store again."

"*Señor* Oliver, I am going to get you something to drink," Rosita said. María retrieved a greasy sofa cushion, which she put behind his head. She found a bit of strong cold coffee that had not spilled. She poured a little of it into a cup and offered it to him. He sipped noisily and seemed to revive.

"What happened to Oliver? Is he all right?" Captain Austin demanded as he came dashing through the saloon.

"I think he hurt his head. He's talking nonsense, *señor*," Rosita said.

Captain Austin crouched on the ground on top of

the papers and said in a loud, deep voice in English, "Oliver, do you hear me? The creditors are after us again. What shall we do?"

Immediately Oliver blinked hard. "Austin, you fool. You don't have to shout."

Captain Austin smiled. He gave Oliver a pat on the shoulder, then turned to Rosita, "He's fine. Don't worry. Now why don't you two come and help me with any other injured passengers. We need to move everybody off the boat."

"Why?" Rosita demanded.

"Lightening," Captain Austin explained. "We need to make the ship lighter to see if we can get off this sandbar."

Until nightfall, Rosita and María helped bandage heads and arms of the injured. María tore sheets into strips for bandages and dipped water. There was so little medicine on board that all Rosita could do was help make people comfortable on the shore. Fortunately, no one was severely injured.

"I'm afraid Rackliffe's gone and done it this time," Oliver said. He sat on a blanket with a bandage Rosita had wrapped around his head. Mosquitoes bit unmercifully, even though fires had been built on shore. "The *Ariel's* stuck good this time, I know it. We'll never get to Matamoros now."

Rosita glanced nervously at the trapped steamboat, which seemed to flounder like a large gasping fish out of water. After it was clear that the unloaded *Ariel* could not back away from the sandbar, Captain Austin came up with another plan. "We'll try warping," he announced.

McCallister ordered Apollo to row the scow with a stout line to the far opposite shore. Apollo secured the line to the biggest tree he could find. Then every man—passenger and crew alike—was ordered to the capstan. The capstan looked like a giant spool that stood upright on deck. Bars were inserted in holes around the top. The other end of the line was wrapped around the middle of the capstan. With great effort the men pushed against the capstan's bars and turned the line round and round the cylinder. Meanwhile, Rackliffe ordered power to the paddle wheels, which attempted to move the boat forward. In spite of all this effort, they could not drag the groaning steamboat over the sandbar.

"Now what'll we do?" McCallister leaned exhausted against the capstan. Night was coming. María glanced nervously at the darkening bluffs. The boat, cargo, and all the passengers were trapped and helpless—perfect prey for *banditos* or Comanche.

"Grasshoppering!" Rackliffe shouted from the pilothouse.

"*¿Como le va?*" María asked Carlos.

"*Saltamontes*," he replied, smiling.

"He says they're going to make the ship into a grasshopper," María told Rosita. Rosita shook her head in amazement. These *norteamericanos!* To transform a boat into a *saltamontes*. Here was something she wanted to see.

McCallister bellowed to the crew, "Nail a broad shoe to the heel of the spar!"

Over the bow, or front of the boat, the crew lifted up two long, stout poles as tall as trees. They attached a flat piece of wood to the end of each pole.

"Set the spars!"

The crew planted each of the long poles, which were called spars, into the sandy mud—"shoe" first. The poles were set on an angle so that the end sticking out of the water sloped toward the boat.

One end of line was lashed to the top of each pole through a special block and wheel and then attached to the bow. The other end of the line was threaded around the capstan. Rosita and María watched in wonder as the crew again began the difficult job of pushing and turning the capstan. As they did, the front end of the steamboat raised up slowly from the sandbar and the entire vessel moved forward a few feet as if it were crawling on long skinny legs.

The boat was lowered, the spars were reset and

the whole procedure was repeated. Hours passed. Little by little the steamboat hobbled forward. Torches burned along the shore and the passengers tried to get what little sleep they could in the open. For the crew, the work was backbreaking and exhausting.

When the steamboat was nearly clear of the sandbar, the tackle snapped. "Watch out!" warned McCallister. The groaning boat pitched to one side. The bow crashed into the water with an awful thud. Bars of the unmanned capstan whirled out of control, hit Carlos, and threw him from the deck. Other men flipped into the water. Screams and shouts for help filled the air.

It was as if in slow motion an enormous, injured animal suddenly and painfully dropped to its knees. McCallister did not hesitate. He waded into the water, shouting orders. Those who were able joined him, searching for bodies, dragging anyone they could find from the dark, shallow current.

Chapter 11

Carlos's arm was badly broken. Another deckhand had bruises and a cut over one eye. A third suffered from broken ribs. The rest of the crew was amazingly whole. Captain Austin had no idea how to medicate the sick or mend the hurt. Carlos, ordinarily amiable, cheerful, and obliging, sat on the shore and held his arm and cried with pain. It was clearly a serious compound fracture, with the bone sticking right through the skin.

The sight of the boy's suffering upset Captain Austin. "I could suggest a powerful dose of calomel of julep and a dose of castor oil. If that doesn't work, perhaps we could try a blister on the chest and then rub his throat with liniment," Captain

Austin said, suggesting every remedy he had ever been given by a doctor.

Rosita recalled vaguely her mother assisting a sheep herder who had a badly broken leg. She volunteered to help Rackliffe, who claimed to know how to set all kinds of bones. María grudgingly said she'd help, too, although she soon regretted the offer. Resetting Carlos's arm by lantern light was a grisly experience that lasted more than an hour. There was no painkiller for Carlos except a few swigs of whiskey. Rackliffe, who finished off the rest of the bottle, seemed almost overcome by the ordeal. His face, normally pale, turned bright red to match his hair. During the operation María fainted—something that McCallister seemed to note.

Rosita, however, remained amazingly calm. She felt as if she were being guided by some other hand, some other voice. Time vanished altogether. She thought neither of herself or what she looked like or what people thought of her. She concentrated completely on the task at hand.

"Bueno. Bueno, señorita," Carlos whispered in a hoarse, grateful voice when it was all over.

To Rosita his words were like a blessing. She smiled, surprised by her own sense of satisfaction. They had done as good a job as they could, considering that she had none of the special aromatic mixture of wild flowers and blessed rosemary wet with alcohol to massage into his shoulder. Silently, she said prayers to the Virgin of Guadalupe to cure him. God willing, Carlos would be all right.

No moon or stars shone overhead. The weary group of travelers on shore were assailed by a steady cloud of mosquitoes. The boat stood tilted on one spar in the middle of the river. Because the boat seemed too unsteady, Captain Austin ordered everyone to spend the night on shore. They had few blankets and no tents. Babies cried. Children whined. Some of the deck passengers quarreled. Several of the disgruntled travelers from cabin class huddled on the shore and complained and schemed.

"We'll walk to Matamoros," the Reverend Spike declared.

"I've had enough," Madame de la Barca muttered.

The Texan with the moustache nodded in agreement. "Take some food, maybe a few guns—we could get there faster than riding on this poor excuse for a boat."

The crew grumbled mutiny, too. Even McCallister, who had bullied and beaten and worked the deck-hands beyond the point of endurance, had decided enough was enough. "Captain's a fool," he hissed to Belknap. "I told him, 'Dump that cussed printing press. Dump the rest of the cargo.' But would he listen to me? Never."

"This mess is Rackliffe's fault. Lucky he didn't kill us all," Belknap said. He looked anxiously at the steamboat and considered how much damage the bow had taken in the crash. Would the boiler even run again?

"We should just throw the cargo overboard. Especially that press. What's the point of books for people who can't read nothing?" McCallister's voice became even lower and more confidential. "I say we get rid of Austin and Oliver. We hold Rackliffe hostage. Then we bandage up the ship and go on. At least we'll have the ship. Maybe there's a chance we can make it. After all, there are more ways to kill a dog than to choke him to death with butter." McCallister winked. "Are you with me?"

Belknap gave the mate a puzzled look. *Get rid of Austin and Oliver?* He was a mechanic, not a mur-derer—in spite of what was said about him and that boiler accident on the steamboat *Trinidad*.

"Well, man, speak up. Don't just sit there like a notch on a stick. Are you with me or no?" McCallister hissed. He knew he couldn't run the ship by himself. Belknap was the only one who could keep this puddle-jumper running. But would he keep his mouth shut when they reached Matamoros?

"What are you two gabbing about?" Captain Austin demanded. He appeared suddenly, hovering over them and their conversation like an enormous blue-bottle fly.

"Nothing," McCallister mumbled. He cleared his throat and gave Belknap a threatening look. "We should throw the cargo overboard, Captain. We'll never get off this sandbar so heavily loaded. The boat's crippled. Especially with that printing press—"

"I won't, sir. Paid more than fifteen hundred dollars for that press. It's worth more than that. Why, the press is worth more than the boat, if you want to know," Captain Austin said in outrage. "Sir, what are you thinking? In the morning things will look better. We'll get off this sandbar. Same as we have before, sir. Mark my words."

McCallister's expression darkened. When Captain Austin turned his back, McCallister sneered. He glanced knowingly at Belknap and drew a finger across his lizard-like neck. Belknap nodded.

That was all that María saw. But it was enough to make her nervous. "*Señor* Austin? What will we do now?" she pleaded. "What will become of us?"

"One thing we won't do is throw my printing

press overboard," Captain Austin grumbled. "I don't care what McCallister says."

When María heard these words, she knew the press was doomed to be eaten by the river. No one on the ship was as powerful as the mate. *"¡No hay mal que por bien no venga!"* she told Rosita. McCallister's words would come to no good. "There is nothing like that printing press in all of *Seno Mexicano*. How can he threaten to throw it overboard?"

Rosita did not answer. She had not paid any attention to her stepsister or the arguments of the passengers and the crew. Instead she was listening for any noise on the bluffs. In the darkness among the trees someone was watching and waiting. She was certain. When she stood to throw another log on the fire, she sensed a subtle movement among the branches. The nearly imperceptible thump of the hoof of a sleek, swift horse. The sad lowing of the *Ariel*'s only milk cow.

"What is wrong?" María asked, her eyes wide with terror.

Rosita put a finger to her mouth. She listened. An owl hooted. Its warning echoed across the river.

Rosita crept to Oliver. The clerk sat hunched forward on a log beside the fire. An old coat was draped around his shoulders. *"Señor,"* she said. "I must speak to you."

"What is it?" He looked up at her with a glance that reminded her of a very young boy. A very frightened young boy.

"Comanche," she whispered. Only her eyes moved, motioning toward the shadowy trees where she sensed horsemen hiding.

Oliver pursed his lips. He nodded briefly and struggled to stand. Then, with as much grace as he could manage, he lumbered over to Captain Austin, who morosely whittled a stick on the other side of the fire. "Did I ever tell you about the time a bunch of Comanche raiders slipped into camp where a dozen men were sleeping?" Oliver said. Sweat beaded on his forehead, yet he spoke casually, as if nothing were wrong. "Each of them carried a rope and had his horse tied to his wrist by a lasso."

Captain Austin glanced with mocking eyes at Oliver. "You never fail to amaze me, sir. Here we are trapped and bewildered. No rescue in sight. And you tell stories. Maybe that crash—"

"Those Comanche were within six feet of the sleepers," Oliver interrupted. Now his glance was desperate. His chins quivered. "The Indians got away with every single horse and did not wake a soul. Not a soul."

Captain Austin closed his pocket knife and replaced it in his pocket. Chuckling, he stood and patted Oliver on the shoulder. "Where are they?" he said between gritted teeth.

"Up the bluff," Oliver replied. "What do we do? The cannons are upended and useless. Who knows if we've even got dry powder. Half the riflemen are injured. The boat's useless. I don't fancy being taken captive, sir. You know what the Comanche do to captives —"

"Stop blubbering, Oliver," Captain Austin replied as calmly as he could. "Let me think." One by one he spoke softly to each member of the crew as if he were making a joke, telling a tale. *"Canción, por favor,"* he whispered to María. "Some pleasant tune to get everyone calmly back on board. We'll just have to pray these Comanche don't speak Spanish."

She looked at him with surprise. He winked. Then she understood. A warning song. Taking a deep breath, she tilted her head back and with her mouth wide open sang *"Los inditos"* in a loud voice.

*"Ahí vienen los inditos
por el carrizal,
ahí vienen los inditos
por el carrizal—"*

When Madame de la Barca and the other passengers heard María's pleasing melody, they stopped talking and listened. Some who knew Spanish began singing along. In small groups these same women and children rose slowly, quietly from the places along the shore. They motioned to the others. They did not panic, even though their expressions were stunned, terrified.

Reverend Spike and the handful of other Texans waded into the water as if nothing were wrong—as if no one were waiting in the trees. They helped the women and children climb aboard the lopsided deck and hide among the helter-skelter boxes and bales. The injured were moved next. The steamboat's remaining upright spar groaned and creaked.

Meanwhile, Austin and McCallister waved their arms to drive the remaining cattle and pigs and sheep and chickens from their makeshift pens to the safety of the trees. In the mad scramble to escape, the trampling animals caused the Comanche a short diversion. One more bit of loot.

In the midst of the chaos María kept singing. She and Rosita crawled on to the ship together. They found an empty space and wedged themselves between a pile of wood and the printing press. Rosita heard McCallister's voice and the click of rifles being loaded.

"Hurry! Come on. Come on!"

Something flashed among the trees illuminated

by the flickering campfire on shore. A silent, bright shape. Then another. Fierce Comanche braves darted among the trees on one side of the river. They wore their long hair parted in the middle, their scalps painted red, their faces decorated with blue and yellow and black and a single feather in their hair. Some had faces tattooed, ears pierced. Around their necks hung deer hooves and many-colored feathers. One wore the woolly horns of a buffalo.

"All hands ready," McCallister growled.

The singing stopped. In the eerie silence Rosita tried to count how many Indians surrounded them, but they moved too quickly, too cautiously. The only light came from the distant flickering of the campfire. No lanterns were lit on the steamboat. Someone on board whimpered.

"Hush!" came a voice.

The waiting went on and on. María squirmed. What were they doing? What were they waiting for? Perhaps the Comanche had heard about the powers of the steamboat. Perhaps they knew of its great booming voice and how it flattened trees with a gun bigger than any rifle ever seen before. Perhaps they were sizing up this strange river creature, waiting for the right moment.

Zizz! Something flamed and arched overhead.

"Fire!" McCallister shouted. The burning arrow landed on the painted canvas roof of the pilothouse. It flickered and smoldered. The bitter smell of smoke filled everyone's nose.

"We're sitting on a pile of kindling!" Belknap hollered. "Now what, Captain?"

Before Captain Austin could answer, another arrow scorched the night sky. This one landed in a cotton bale, which exploded into flames. "All hands!" McCallister shouted. Passengers and crew alike began beating the bale with whatever they could find—sacks, coats, aprons—and dashing out the flame with buckets of river water.

Chapter

12

"We will all be killed," Rosita murmured, too stunned to do anything except watch the others on board race back and forth frantically pushing the burning bale off the deck into the river before the other bales caught fire. "I wish I had never left home. I wish—"

"No time for wishes," María said angrily. "You know what to do."

"What do you mean?" Rosita gulped.

Another arrow. This one missed its target and landed just a few feet away in the water. It sizzled and vanished.

María grabbed Rosita's arm and dragged her into hiding behind the barrel. "The only way we will ever be freed again is if you use some special chants for rain," she said.

"What are you saying?" Rosita looked at her stepsister with suspicion.

Someone screamed. This time the arrow landed in the stern among crates filled with bolts of calico and whiskey. The wooden boxes smoldered then burst into flames. McCallister shouted to the deckhands.

"Rain will put out the fire," María told Rosita. "Rain will raise the boat. Rain will free us."

Rosita's eyes narrowed. "You think it is so easy to invite the rain?"

"I know you can do it. Surely Tía Lupe must have shown you. Everyone says—"

"What do you or anyone else in Guerrero really know about Tía Lupe?" Rosita said fiercely.

"Do something. Do something now!" Rosita begged.

Rosita did not move. She did not speak.

From shore came another burst of laughter. The Comanche howled with delight as another arrow zipped through the air and exploded in flames upstairs in the saloon where the carpeting was already smoldering.

"The chant! Please begin the chant," María pleaded. With every arrow, another fire began. Now there were too many to keep under control. "Certainly you must remember something."

Rosita closed her eyes. She tried to remember the songs her mother hummed to her when she was little. They were powerful songs, she knew, but she was so young. Now she wished she had paid better attention. She hummed and hummed.

Nothing happened.

"Is that the best you can do?" María said desperately.

"I'm trying. *Por favor*. Give me a chance," Rosita replied with irritation.

"Perhaps it is a song of Tía Lupe. Perhaps if you imagined rain in your head," María suggested. She stomped on a burning scrap of cloth blown their way by the wind.

Rosita tried to think of Tía Lupe's strange songs. She imagined great gray curtains of cool rain. She tried to feel pattering drops against her eyelids, her forehead.

Nothing happened.

"Lightning and thunder. Can you see them? Can you hear them in your head? Concentrate," María pleaded. "Please concentrate."

Rosita tried. She focused all her energy on Tía Lupe and rain, on Tía Lupe and cloud, on Tía Lupe and wind.

There was an explosion of gunfire in the bow. But Rosita did not stop. She kept imagining the way the great bruise-colored rain clouds rolled over the plains, blocking the sun. How they pushed stinging dust and sand ahead of them in a cool, billowing wave that bent the mesquite.

María felt a rumble. *Is it the boiler?* The boat seemed to shake. Now they were done for certainly. If the boiler exploded—

Suddenly something shimmered and pelted on the ship's cabin roof. Something danced and pecked and hammered the deck. The downpour was so abrupt, so complete, so shattering that for a split second no one on board knew what it was.

Rain!

The deluge pounded the ship and made the river dance. Rain put out the fires on the roof, the deck. Thunder grumbled. Wind howled. The ship rocked. Lightning tore great gaps in the night sky. In these brief flashes of terrifying light and noise, María saw Rosita, her eyes still closed, still concentrating.

"Rosita, stop!" she said and pulled her stepsister to her feet. Their clothes were soaked. Rain plastered their hair to the sides of their faces. The first rain in months streamed in their ears, their eyes. Rosita and her stepsister joined the rest of *Ariel's* crew and passengers, who cheered and danced as if they'd never seen a cloudburst or smelled the wondrous green fragrance of rain hitting dust and creosote bush.

The boat rocked and drifted. The spar fell forward as the boat was lifted by the sudden downriver rush of water and freed at last from the sandbar. There was no more firing from shore. No more sign of the Comanche. Captain Austin jumped about like a wet rooster. He took dripping Oliver by the arm and swung him round and round, hooting and hollering. Carlos leapt to his feet and did a kind of joyous rain dance. María applauded and stamped and splashed in a puddle on the deck.

"It's a gully-washer and a fence-lifter!" McCallister crowed, his face streaming wet. "It's raining bull frogs and heifer yearlings!"

Rackliffe, his shirt plastered to his back, danced Rosita around and around in circles until she felt sick with dizziness. He gave her a hard kiss on her damp cheek. She blushed angrily. "Matamoros!" he bellowed in her ear.

"Matamoros!" McCallister echoed.

"If she floats," Belknap muttered. He sensed the ship bob and shift and turn. The river was rising rapidly. Too rapidly. He rushed to the boiler and called to Apollo. "Wood!" he shouted and clanged a warning bell. "Fire her up!"

Torches were lit. The torches sputtered in the heavy rain as they were swung out on long iron arms over the bow. Smoke belched from the smokestack.

"To your station, Mr. Rackliffe," Captain Austin announced. "Hold to the channel, sir. Keep to the outside of the bends and profit by this deep and swift current till we're out of danger."

Chapter
13

All night the rain fell. After anchoring among some trees on a small island, the exhausted passengers and crew of the *Ariel* awoke the next morning to discover that the islands had vanished underwater. Only the strongest, tallest trees remained. And still the rain fell.

Water leaked through the ceiling of the damaged saloon. The few cabin roofs that had not been wrecked by fire offered little protection from the downpour. Below on the main deck shivering, wet passengers had cleared away as much burned debris as they could by simply throwing it overboard. With the cattle gone, there was more room on deck but the open cattle pen had become slippery with puddles, floating manure, and hay.

Wind sent slanted sheets of spray into even the few dry spaces left on board. Shivering deck passengers hugged the wall of the boiler area. All night long Apollo and several other deckhands took turns manning the pumps as water flooded through holes in the hull.

The rain, which had been viewed as a blessing, was now seen as a curse.

"We have got to repair the ship," Belknap told Captain Austin. "I can't do anything till we find a gently sloping gravel beach. Someplace we can safely draw her out of the water and expose the larboard side."

Captain Austin exhaled slowly. "How long will that take?"

"Two days maybe and one night if we get everyone to help. Crew and passengers."

But the passengers had other ideas. Madame de la Barca and her little son and maid had no intention of staying aboard the *Ariel* any longer than necessary. As soon as they reached Mier the next day, she barked at Apollo, "Row us to shore." The Reverend Spike and all the other passengers in cabin class followed her example. The bedraggled, hungry families from deck class were last to be taken ashore in the scow by Apollo. They had little in the way of belongings as they made their way across the boisterous current and buffeting waves. Even Carlos decided to take his chances back on dry land again. He cheerfully said goodbye to María and Rosita before he left on the scow's last run to shore.

The *Ariel* bounced and rolled as Rackliffe blew the steam whistle to attract new customers. But there were few passengers interested in making the last leg of the trip south even after the rain cleared. Mier had been devastated by the sudden flood. Most of the crops had been washed away. Five people had drowned when an embankment caved in and washed away.

An inhabitant of Mier waved his sombrero in the air to signal the boat. "Captain, someone wants to come aboard," Rackliffe called below.

"Send the scow over," Captain Austin replied in a discouraged voice. There were few food supplies left on board. They had hardly any cash and little in the way of cargo to trade for goods and materials needed to make the next leg of the journey upriver.

"*Señor?*" the stranger in the sombrero called from the scow as soon as Apollo managed to tie it up to the *Ariel*. "Have you seen two young girls?"

When Rosita heard the man's voice, she recognized it instantly. *Octavio.* He had followed the river all this long way to find them. Desperately, Rosita dragged her stepsister out of sight behind a barrel. They listened, shivering.

"Who are you? What is your business?" Captain Austin demanded.

"I am Octavio, the servant of don Treviño. I am looking for the daughters of my master, who is desperate to find them."

"What makes you think that they are on my ship?" Captain Austin asked warily.

"I have been searching many leagues for many days. Please understand their father suffers much from a broken heart. He is ill and nearly dying. Someone up river told me that he heard music on the river. The sound of a violin. Let me come aboard."

Ill and nearly dying. Rosita shuddered to think such terrible news might be true. She had broken her father's heart.

"Many passengers have come and gone," Captain Austin replied with irritation. He glanced in the direction of the leaking bow. "Sir, I have my own problems. I cannot keep track of where my customers come from, where they are going. Their family difficulties are of no concern to me, sir."

"*Por favor, señor,*" Octavio pleaded. "Tell me if you have seen such girls on the river. One is very lovely to behold. The other is very plain and younger. You must understand they mean everything to their father. He has one other daughter, recently married to a powerful hacienda owner. There is a handsome reward for their return. Please, *señor,* can you help me find them?"

"A reward?" Captain Austin's expression brightened. "How much?"

"Three hundred pesos."

Captain Austin put his hands behind him and rocked back on his heels. "I am a father, too, sir. And I know what it is like to have a wayward daughter. But I do not think anyone on this ship fits your description." Still Octavio would not budge from the scow. Impatiently, Austin scratched his forehead. "I must go ashore for supplies. You may come aboard and I will leave you in the care of my mate, Mr. McCallister." He signalled to McCallister and explained what the old Mexican wanted.

Immediately, McCallister's beady eyes brightened. He whispered something to Captain Austin.

"Climb aboard, sir," Captain Austin said to the stranger, who was beginning to turn green with seasickness. "Wait here for a moment until my mate returns."

Captain Austin lowered himself into the scow and ordered Apollo to row to shore, leaving Octavio shivering on the steamboat deck.

Meanwhile, before Rosita could creep from her hiding place and run to Octavio, rough hands grabbed her and her stepsister and covered their mouths. "Not a very convincing disguise, *José*," McCallister hissed in María's ear. He held one girl under each of his bulging arms, a wide, dirty palm clasped firmly over each girl's mouth. "Up you go," he said, dragging them up the steps as if they were no heavier than bags of cornmeal. He shoved them both inside the galley. "Stay in here till I say you can come out. There are ways to make a rich father pay more than a few hundred pesos for a ransom." He quickly slammed and bolted the galley door from the outside.

Rosita kicked and pounded the door. María shouted for help. No one could hear them over the roar of the boiler, the rush of the paddle wheels, and the shrieking of the steam whistle. McCallister scurried below deck and spoke in gruff English to bewildered Octavio. "As you can see," he told Octavio, "we've had some Indian attacks. The empty cabins and saloon are so badly burned on the next deck, I can't show them to you safely."

Octavio did not understand what McCallister was saying. All that he could tell was that there were no passengers anywhere in sight as he picked his way around the debris scattered on the main deck. He sighed and made a polite bow. It was clear

151 ❧

that this great steamboat was in terrible disorder. Water sloshed around his ankles as he nervously made his way across the deck. Who could travel safely on such a thing?

He was glad when Apollo returned to row him back to solid land so that he could return to his familiar village. He thanked Captain Austin and was rowed back to Mier. Now Octavio faced the difficult task of telling his master, don Treviño, that his worst fears had been realized. He would never see his beloved Rosita or his stepdaughter María again.

While Captain Austin was gone, McCallister hurried to the boiler room to tell Belknap the clever thing that he had done.

Belknap was not impressed. "Why didn't you simply exchange them for the money outright?" he demanded. "Don't you know kidnapping is illegal? Why hold out for more money when we could use the money from the reward now?"

"That simple servant didn't have the cash necessary to pay a reward," McCallister replied angrily. "I'm no fool. After we take over the ship, we'll take these daughters of Treviño north on our next run to Guerrero. We'll hold them till he meets our price. In the meantime, they'll serve as cook and steward. It's a perfect plan."

Belknap shook his head. "You told me yourself that there were plenty of armed men in Guerrero. You're taking a stupid risk."

McCallister snorted. "I know what I'm doing." He smacked his big, meaty hands together. "I understand the Mexican character completely."

Belknap winced. He bent over and clutched his stomach.

"You don't look good," McCallister said nervously. He needed Belknap for his plan to work. Belknap was the only one who could keep the boiler running.

"I'm fine," Belknap replied. "It's nothing." He bit his lip and hobbled over to a clanking pipe and gave it a loud rap with a wrench.

Rosita and María crouched on the greasy floor of the dark, windowless galley for hours. They had tried kicking and pushing and throwing themselves against the door. It would not budge. Their eyes had finally grown accustomed to the lack of light and now they could see the mice that scrambled up the walls and skittered across the casks of cornmeal and rice. The steamboat rumbled along again on its way to Carmargo.

"We will never escape," Rosita said. Her voice sounded dull and hopeless.

María put her face in her hands and began to sob. *A handsome reward.* Perhaps her stepfather loved her more than she had imagined. And now she would never be able to go home. She would never see him or her mother or her sister again. "What will become of us?"

Rosita did not reply. She thought of her father, ill in his bed. His heart broken. What if at this very moment he was returning from days of nothing but wanderings in his head? She imagined him opening his eyes and looking about his bedroom. Sunlight danced on the clean floor through the open window. From outside came the sounds of children's voices. A bird sang a frail-throated song in his favorite fragrant oleander tree.

"Rosita?" she could hear her father calling like a sharp wind. "Rosita?"

María blew her nose loudly. The sound startled Rosita from her daydream. "We must go back to Guerrero," Rosita said. "There is not a moment to lose."

María looked at her stepsister in amazement. "You speak foolishness. There is no escape from this place. We are prisoners held for ransom."

A mouse leapt from cask to cask with a meager scrap in its mouth. Then it vanished.

María dabbed her eyes with her sleeve. "We shall

grow old aboard the *Ariel*. We will be trapped here for the rest of our lives. Unless, of course, the boiler explodes. Unless, of course, the ship—"

"Be quiet, María. I am trying to think."

María was silent. Another mouse scampered past their feet. "You could use some other chant. You could get us out of here if you tried. Look what happened when you called the rain."

"A flood," Rosita said miserably.

María rubbed her forehead with her finger. She wanted to be helpful. "I heard once that Tía Lupe knew how to find an invisible bone in cats. The most powerful bone of all. I heard that Tía Lupe alone knew how to boil a cat alive, sort through the remains with a mirror. Whatever bone she could not see in the mirror was the one that was invisible. A lucky charm. The most powerful bone of all. Perhaps you have this bone. Perhaps you can use it now."

Rosita shook her head angrily. "What do you know of Tía Lupe? Nothing. Just like everyone else. The villagers called her *bruja* because she was different. Because she lived alone. They blamed her for everything that went wrong." Rosita took a deep breath. "She was my friend."

"I did not mean to speak ill of her," María mumbled.

It's all crazy, Rosita thought. The same people who

cursed Tía Lupe came to her mother for tea of
estrella de anis to calm the itch; or infusions of *gordo
lobo*, fat wolf, when they were sick with fever; or
manzanilla tea when they could not sleep. "María,"
Rosita demanded, "do you know how Tía Lupe
died?"

"I have heard something of it," María replied in a
small, nervous voice. Everyone in Guerrero still
talked about how Juan López was the one who
caught Tía Lupe, because only someone named
Juan is capable of catching a witch. They said
Juan turned his clothes inside out one night and
drew a circle in Tía Lupe's doorway when she was
gone, roaming in the form of an owl or most likely a
coyote. The next day fishermen found her dead
body floating in the river. She was in her human
form, the fishermen said. And their voices were
glad.

"There is a fine line between being a healer and
being a *bruja*," Rosita said. "My mother was always
very careful. She refused to treat people who came
to her with bewitchment. She did not demand sub-
stantial payment for her herbs and secret teas. And
always she had the confidence of the villagers, who
trusted her goodness and her truthfulness. She was
an upright woman."

"I know. Of course, of course. She was a won-

derful person. Please, can you begin the chant?"
María begged.

"As for Tía Lupe—now that was another story.
When women carrying babies passed her they
feared *mal ojo* and they touched their babies' fore-
heads and whispered, *'Dios te guarde, tan lindo,'* so
that God would keep their pretty babies safe. Of
course Tía Lupe did nothing to dispel their fears. If
someone broke out in a fever after mistreating her
or looking too steadily into her rheumy eyes, she
would accept payment to come to their home and
lay hands upon them to take away the spell." Rosita
paused and took a deep breath. "I can not use the
powers of a *bruja* again. I used them once and that
was enough."

"You are very powerful. You could free us."

"And then what? The power becomes a habit.
That is not how I wish to live. That is not how I
wish to die. There are other ways to use what I
know. My mother's ways."

María shivered. She had never thought that a gift
might also be a kind of burden. She sighed. Rosita
was stubborn. María would never convince her to
use a *bruja* spell. They would have to think of some
other way to escape. But what?

Absentmindedly, María watched the mouse stop
and clean its whiskers with its small gray paws.

"*¡Hola!*" María said. At the sound of her greeting, the mouse dashed up the wall and through a hole in the corner of the ceiling.

Rosita jumped to her feet. She pushed a barrel into the corner of the galley, stood on it, and tried to reach the ceiling with her outstretched hand.

"What are you doing?" María demanded. Was Rosita *loca?*

"Hand me a wooden spoon. The one with the long handle."

"You are not going to cook now, are you?" María unhooked the spoon from the opposite wall.

Rosita did not answer. She took the spoon and poked it into the hole. The damp rotten boards were as soft as a soggy tortilla. She pried the spoon like a lever. A whole section of board bent toward her. She pulled this away with her hands. Above she could see the thin layer of worn, painted canvas that covered the roof. "Give me that knife," Rosita said. She used the knife that María gave her to pry away more rotten ceiling board. Carefully, she left the topmost canvas layer in place.

"Hurry!" María whispered. She glanced nervously toward the door. What if McCallister came back and saw what Rosita was doing?

"Stay by the door and listen for footsteps," Rosita said. She peeled another handful of slivered ceiling away. The opening was almost big enough. The boat shuddered, slowed, and then the noisy engine stopped. All was quiet.

"Footsteps!" María hissed. "Someone's coming."

In her hurry to climb off the barrel, Rosita knocked over a tin of hardtack from the shelf. The tin crashed on the floor. Crackers rolled everywhere.

"What's going on in there?" McCallister's voice rumbled in English on the other side of the door. There was the brisk sound of the door being unbolted. Light suddenly flooded the galley.

Chapter 14

"Buenos días, señor," María mumbled to McCallister.

The mate glared at the girls as they tried to gather up the hardtack. "Can't understand me, can you?"

Rosita looked up at him and said sweetly, *"Sí, señor puerco."*

María bit her lip to keep from grinning.

"No use trying to tell you more than half the crew's sick. Doubled over with vomiting and stomach cramps. Rackliffe included. Now we've got enough water to float upriver but nobody to run this boat."

Rosita smiled. *"Sí, señor."*

McCallister let out a great breath of air. "I'll never understand you ignorant Mexicans," he said with disgust. "Captain says for me to give you this.

Thinks maybe you'll know what to do. The man hasn't got as much sense as last year's bird nest with the bottom punched out." He handed Rosita a torn page from what looked like a ledger book. Faded blue writing marked the creased page, water stained and grubby from handling.

Rosita looked at the strange foreign words in puzzlement. Then she passed the piece of paper to María. The page said:

```
I part laudanum
I   "   camphorated spirits
2   "   capsicum
2   "   tinctur'd ginger


Dose for an adult is ½ teaspoonful in a wine glass of
water. If the case is severe or obstinate repeat the dose
in three or four hours.
```

María shook her head. She could not understand the English words. She gave the page back to McCallister. *"Lo siento, señor."*

"Knew it'd be no use trying. Just as well go out and bay at the moon." McCallister folded up the remedy recipe and stuffed it into his pocket. "Now back you go, little ladies." He pointed to the galley. "Why don't you fix up some vittles for me and

Apollo, seeing as how we're the only ones left aboard who aren't sick as dogs?"

Rosita didn't want to be locked up again. She put her hands on her hips and held her ground stubbornly.

McCallister made a motion as if he were stirring something in a bowl. He pointed to Rosita and her stepsister. He pointed to the galley. With a shoveling motion, he pretended to eat.

Now Rosita understood. *"Sí, señor puerco,"* she said. *";Cuche cuche cochino!"*

María covered her mouth to muffle her laugh.

McCallister nodded with a nasty grin. "Now fix up some grub before I knock you sky-westward and crooked eastward. And don't be thinking about running away, *comprendes?* I'm watching you. You two's worth a lot of money." He took a seat at the opposite end of the saloon. He tilted back in the battered chair and began cleaning his fingernails with a knife. There was nothing else he could do since Belknap was so sick. He couldn't run the steamboat alone. He'd just have to be patient. Belknap was a tough old bird. He'd pull through. As for the others, there were ways to make sure they didn't survive. And no one would suspect anything. That was the beauty of it.

"Very clever, Rosita," María whispered. "I'm

glad he doesn't know the call used to feed pigs back in—"

"Shshshshs!" Rosita said. She cocked her head to one side. There was something very odd happening on board the *Ariel*. It was far too quiet. Where was everyone? Except for McCallister and Apollo, there were no deckhands to be seen scurrying about the cabin deck. Even the engines were eerily silent. Rosita handed her stepsister a bucket and told her to get some fresh water and kindling. "Gather up all our things. The violin, your book," she whispered. "You and I are leaving soon."

McCallister looked up from his fingernails. "What about that grub?"

"*Sí, señor,*" Rosita said. She motioned for her stepsister to hurry.

"Where you think you're going?" McCallister demanded.

María motioned with the bucket to show that she meant to gather water from the river. He nodded. While María went downstairs to the main deck, Rosita picked up a broom and swept hardtack crumbs from the galley floor into the saloon. As she did, she peeked in the nearby cabin. There she saw Rackliffe in the bed, his face pale, his hair even brighter than usual. She kept sweeping. The next cabin, with a great gap in the roof, was occupied by

Oliver, who groaned loudly. The room smelled putrid. "Are you ill, *señor?*" she asked, holding her nose.

Oliver's eyes opened wide when he heard her voice. "I'm afraid it is the cholera," he replied in Spanish.

When Rosita heard these words, she took a step backward. The same disease had ravaged her little village five years ago. Nearly twenty people had died. Among them was her mother, who caught the illness while caring for the sick.

"*Por favor,*" Oliver begged weakly. "A tincture of camphor, peppermint, and asafetida. One-half teaspoon every hour."

Rosita bit her lip. "I do not have such medicines." In Guerrero they used *gordo lobo*, rice water, special incense, and prayers. But even those did not always work.

"Little lady?" McCallister bellowed from the saloon. "I'm not a high flung fellow when it comes to waiting for vittles."

"*Sí, señor,*" Rosita answered impatiently. She turned to Oliver. She did not want to help him. Her own father was ill and might die before she reached him. She and María had to escape from this boat. There was not a moment to lose.

Oliver winced. He shut his eyes and his mouth

twitched. Then he bent double so that all the sheets in the bed twisted. "Help me. Oh, please help me," he whispered in English.

Rosita heard her stepsister's quick, light footsteps hurrying up the stairway with fresh water. Rosita sighed. She lifted Oliver's head and turned over the grimy pillow. She straightened the sheets. Oliver looked at her with dull, glassy eyes. She tried not to breathe through her nose.

"What do you want me to do now?" María whispered from Oliver's doorway. "They're all sick. Everyone except Apollo and McCallister. Now's our best chance to get out of here. We can take the scow to shore tonight when they're sleeping."

"Start the fire in the stove. Set a kettle on to boil," Rosita replied.

"You're not listening," María replied angrily. "We've got to get out of here. Tonight may be our only chance."

Rosita pursed her lips. "Pick the bugs from the rice. Add plenty of water and cook it up."

María grumbled as she stirred a thin, watered-down corn gruel in a pan for McCallister and Apollo. Rosita dipped a cloth in the cool water. She washed Oliver's feverish face. Carefully, she lifted his head and gave him a few sips of rice water and wiped his chin. He murmured something she could not understand, shut his eyes, and went to sleep. Rosita did the same for each of the ill crew members.

"All hands! All hands!" Captain Austin mumbled in delirium. Apollo leaned against the captain's cabin wall. He watched Rosita trying to spoon rice water into his master's mouth. When Captain Austin knocked the spoon from her hand, Apollo bent over and picked it up. He held it just out of her reach. "Spoon?" he said in English.

"Por favor," Rosita said impatiently.

"Spoon? *En español, por favor,"* he asked.

Now she understood. *"Cuchara,"* she replied.

"Cuchara." Apollo smiled and gave her the spoon. *"Gracias."*

That evening the river rolled brown and muddy and strong. On the main deck ankle deep water sloshed near the bow. Wearily, Rosita dumped the dirty pans into a tub of water in the saloon. She looked down at her grimy, calloused hands. Her hair smelled greasy and hung in lank strands at each side of her face. When she glanced at her own reflection in the saloon's broken mirror, she hardly recognized herself. Dark circles rimmed her eyes. Her mouth looked strangely puffy. She was gaunt and hollow-cheeked. No one in Guerrero would recognize her.

"The book, the violin," María whispered. She

pointed to an old burlap feed sack in a corner of the galley. "They are safe."

"And the scow?" Rosita said in a low voice. "Where is it?"

María looked nervously over her shoulder. "Tied up beside the boat. Not far from the wheel house on the starboard side."

Heavy footsteps rumbled across the saloon floor. "Well, little ladies. Time for you to say good night," McCallister announced. He motioned toward the galley, where he clearly meant to lock them up again.

Rosita hoped her anxious gaze would not betray their escape route through the galley's ceiling. She knew they were somehow going to climb up through the roof and crawl outside on top of the steamboat. From there they'd have to lower themselves down, unseen, into the scow. But how? She had not thought of that part of the plan. With no rope, no ladder it seemed impossible.

"*Señor?*" Rosita said, desperate to stall McCallister.

"Now what?" he demanded.

She gulped.

"What do you want?"

She could not understand him. He could not understand her. She motioned desperately toward the galley. She tilted her head, held her hands palms together and placed them beside one cheek to indicate sleep. Then she shook her head vigorously.

"Well, don't that beat a hen a-scratchin'!" McCallister exclaimed. "You're such a fancy lady you think the bare galley floor's not good enough for the likes of you to spend the night." He grabbed a few mildewed wool blankets from one of the cabins and handed them gruffly to Rosita. "It's a good thing I'm such a thoughtful gentleman. Don't you agree?"

"*Sí, señor,*" Rosita replied as sweetly as she could. She motioned to her stepsister to hurry into the galley before McCallister changed his mind about being so generous. The door slammed shut and was bolted from the outside.

Rosita whispered her idea to María. María sang loudly as they tore the blanket into many strips. There was a loud knock at the door. The girls froze. A deep voice growled, "Shut up, will you?"

"*Sí, señor,*" Rosita replied, started by the sharp warning in McCallister's voice. She gathered up the cut-up pieces of blanket and tried desperately to hide them behind her. When McCallister walked away, she and María breathed a sigh of relief. Silently, they tied the strips of blanket together.

María climbed atop the barrels balanced in the corner. She carried the long string of blanket over one shoulder. "Careful," Rosita whispered. She handed her a kitchen knife. María reached up and slit the blade up into the corner of the ceiling, piercing the canvas covering. She held the knife in her teeth as she pulled away more soggy, rotten canvas with both hands. She slipped the knife up through the hole and lay it on the roof. Then she pulled herself up through the hole by gripping tightly to what was left of a few wooden crossbeams.

She grunted as she flopped on to her stomach and awkwardly kicked and pushed and pulled so that she had slithered completely out on to the roof. Wind blew in her hair and cooled her sweaty face. Her heart thumped wildly. No lantern burned in the pilothouse. To be safe, she kept herself low on the roof. The river grumbled. On shore flickered a few lights. What if someone in Camargo heard them? What if—

"María!" Rosita whispered anxiously. María leaned into the hole and pulled up the sack. With great effort, she helped hoist Rosita on to the roof as well. The canvas and boards creaked. Without speaking, they crept to the roof edge on the starboard side. The scow was tied beside the steamboat in the water below.

María knotted one end of the blanket rope to a secure pipe leading to the pilothouse. She dropped the other end of the makeshift rope over the edge of the roof. Was it strong enough? "Careful," she said softly to Rosita, who handed her the burlap sack. "You bring the knife."

"How?" Rosita asked nervously.

"In your teeth," María whispered. She poked her arm through a hole in the burlap and then wrapped the sack over one shoulder as if it were a *rebozo*. She held her breath and lowered her feet over the edge of the roof, gripping the rope tightly with both hands. Silently, she prayed that she would not wake McCallister, who was snoring in the saloon below.

Inch by inch she shimmied down the rope. Past the second deck slowly, slowly to the main deck. In the darkness she heard the scow bump against the steamboat. A few more inches. A few more.

The bag slipped from her shoulder. *My book!* She grabbed. Too late! *Splash!* The bag vanished. In that instant, she lost her grip on the rope. She clawed at the side of the boat. She plunged and vanished into the dark river.

María! Holding the knife in her teeth, Rosita scrambled over the roof's edge and down the rope. Her hands burned. Her skirt tangled around her knees. Before she reached the scow she heard another loud *splash!* She jumped into the scow, cut the rope with the knife. She tossed the knife into the bottom of the boat. Quickly, she grabbed the oars and pulled.

"Who goes there?" McCallister's voice boomed from the *Ariel*. "Apollo?"

Rosita hunched forward and kept rowing. Lantern light bobbed on the steamboat's main deck. Desperately, she scanned the dark river in hopes of hearing the thrashing of her stepsister in the water. Anything—any sign at all. The scow plunged and bucked. She could not control its direction. The current was too strong. She yanked the oars. Sweat ran down her face. She rowed and rowed but did not seem to be getting anywhere. "María!" she called. How long could her stepsister survive in the water? Rosita could hear nothing. She could see nothing.

When she glanced for one split second at the anchored *Ariel*, the lantern light seemed to have grown fainter, smaller. Was she being swept upstream? That was impossible. Frantic and confused, Rosita pulled harder. She called, "María! Where are you?"

Only the river answered.

Chapter 15

After what seemed forever, Rosita struggled to shore. The scow bumped against the soft embankment among slimy driftwood. In a daze she crawled out of the boat and waded through the shallow water to dry land. When she turned to look out over the river, the *Ariel* had disappeared. She felt as if she had been awakened from a dream. Had she really been aboard the steamboat? Had her sister fallen into the water—or was this, too, part of some terrible nightmare?

Desperately, she sloshed again up to her knees into the current. Her soggy, dirty skirt wound around her legs. "María!" she called. "María!"

No answer.

Rosita hugged her arms and shivered, watching,

waiting. *I should have gone first.* Maybe none of this would have happened if she had been the first one down that rope. She could have helped María. María would be safe. She should never have allowed María to go first. *Never.*

Frogs croaked. Biting mosquitoes whined around her face. The humid, heavy air felt suffocating. She could hardly breathe. She could hardly think. What should she do? She slapped at something nipping her leg. She had to stay here until morning. Perhaps then she would find María. *Yes.* Perhaps her stepsister had somehow managed to survive. Perhaps she grabbed a wrack-pile, a tree limb. Perhaps she was safe asleep on a river bank. That was why she could not hear Rosita calling her name.

She tried to feel hopeful. She tried to imagine María safe. But deep down she knew. The Río Bravo had taken María.

Splash!

Rosita held her breath. She listened. Were her ears deceiving her?

Splash!

"María!" she screamed.

A tall, hulking shape sloshed through the shallows toward her. Coughing. Falling to its knees.

"Apollo?" she called, amazed.

He stumbled up the riverbank and collapsed on the muddy ground, too weak to speak. When she leaned over him, she could hear him breathing. Great wheezing gasps.

He was still alive.

Apollo could not tell Rosita how he had cut the anchor to the *Ariel* and set the steamboat adrift before he plunged into the water after María. He could not tell her how desperately he swam when the current sucked him under. He could not tell her how he nearly drowned trying to make it to shore.

Yet somehow Rosita understood that he had tried to save María. And he, too, had failed.

Now he slept.

Near the river's edge Rosita crouched filled with misery and loneliness. Pain twisted slowly in her chest. *Is this what a broken heart feels like?* Without really thinking what she was doing, she began to sing. A strange haunting song about partners in time, fellow travelers, and witnesses. Her chant echoed up and down the river. Raising his head for a moment, Apollo listened, half-asleep and half-dreaming. Rosita sang and sang, never stopping once. Her eyes closed, she saw nothing, heard nothing except the song for her stepsister.

Slowly, imperceptibly at first, the sky lightened. Above the low flat eastern horizon vapory clouds glowed pink then orange then pink again. The river turned deep umber. Someone touched Rosita's arm. She opened her eyes. It was Apollo. He pointed to the nearby trees along the river's edge.

María staggered toward them through the underbrush.

Dumbfounded, Rosita rubbed her eyes. "*Sueño*," she murmured. What else could it be?

But as María came closer and closer, Rosita could see with her own eyes, she could hear with her own ears that this was no dream. Rosita stood, ran to María, and embraced her. For a very long time, she could not speak.

"Your song," María whispered, exhausted. Her face was muddy, her clothing torn. "I was in the water. Swept away. Then I heard your song. And somehow I managed to come ashore. I don't know how." She tried to catch her breath. "Upriver. I was walking, crawling. I don't know. It was your voice I was following. The voice of a powerful *curandera*."

Rosita looked at her stepsister in surprise and wonder. What if she were right? What if her song had saved her?

María sighed. "Your violin, my book—gone forever. I am sorry."

"They are not as important as what is not lost."

María looked confused. "And what is that?"

"You," Rosita said, smiling. "The brave singer of *corridos.*" She paused. "Are you ready? We have a long way to travel home. We might still arrive in time to help Papa."

María motioned to Apollo. "You come, too." She pointed to him and then to herself and her stepsister. *"Casa,"* she told him.

Apollo nodded. Clearly, they were inviting him to their house. All right, he'd get them back safely upriver to their folks. Maybe he'd stay a few days. And then he'd be on his way before Austin or any other slave-catchers came looking for him. He'd find a place small and remote in Mexico—far away from Texas. *"Libertad,"* he said, grinning.

"Libertad," María said in a voice filled with gladness. Freedom. She had not taught him that word. He had learned it on his own.

Together they walked along the edge of the Río Bravo upriver the way they had come. "Someday you and I will go to the sea," María promised Rosita.

"Tell us of the sea," Rosita said.

And María began to make up a new ballad. She sang this *corrido* as they walked back to Guerrero. Neither María, Rosita, nor Apollo noticed that following them at a respectful distance through the mesquite along the river's edge was another traveler. A yellow-eyed coyote.

Author's Note

Captain Henry Austin might have renamed the Río Grande the River of Lost Dreams. In 1830, after a series of economic disasters, he abandoned the Río Grande and sold his printing press for scrap. The *Ariel* eventually limped up the coast to the Brazos River in August 1830, and Austin attempted to go upriver in it to the town of Brazoria. This, too, ended in failure when the *Ariel* hit a sandbar. Stubbornly, Austin sent the damaged *Ariel* into the Atlantic Ocean to sail to New Orleans. After three unsuccessful attempts to reach the United States, the *Ariel* ended her days in Galveston Bay. She sank and was abandoned somewhere near the mouth of the San Jacinto River. It would be sixteen years before steamboats returned to the Río Grande.

As for the fate of the village of Guerrero, it, too, would be plagued by the river. In 1953, in a misguided attempt to control the Río Grande and promote irrigation and tourism, the United States and Mexico signed a treaty to create the Falcon Dam. Guerrero was one of many towns that had be abandoned by residents when the dam flooded 114,000 acres of land to create a new, artificial lake. Guerrero ended under the waters of the Río Grande, just as the old curse had predicted: *"Terminará bajo las aguas."*

Bibliography

Baker, T. Lindsay and Julie P. *Till Freedom Cried Out: Memories of Texas Slave Life.* College Station, TX: Texas A&M University Press, 1997.

Berlandier, Jean Louis. *Journey to Mexico During the Years 1826 to 1834.* Austin, TX: Texas State Historical Association.

Boatright, Mody C., editor. *Texas Folk and Folklore.* Dallas: Southern Methodist University Press, 1954.

Calderone, Fanny de la Barca. *Life in Mexico.* New York: E.P. Dutton and Co. Inc., 1946.

Deutsch, Sarrah. *No Separate Refuge: Culture, Class and Gender.* New York: Oxford University Press, 1987.

Dobie, J. Frank, editor. *Southwestern Lore,* No. IX,

Publications of the Texas Folk-Lore Society. Dallas: Southwest Press, 1931.

Fehrenbach, T.R. *Fire & Blood: A History of Mexico*. New York: DaCapo Press, 1995.

Fergusson, Harvey. *Río Grande*. New York: Alfred A. Knopf, 1933.

García, Rogelia O. *Dolores, Revilla and Laredo: Three Sister Settlements*, Privately printed, Laredo, TX, 1970.

Gilpin, Laura. *The Rio Grande: River of Destiny.* New York: Duell, Sloan and Pearce, 1949.

Horgan, Paul. *Great River: The Río Grande in History*. Hanover, NH: Wesleyan University Press, 1984.

Huddleston, Duane, editor. *Steamboats and Ferries on the White River*. Fayetteville, AK: University of Arkansas Press, 1998.

Hunter, Louis C. *Steamboats on the Western Rivers*. New York: Dover Publications, Inc., 1993.

Kelley, Pat. *River of Lost Dreams: Navigation on the Río Grande*. Lincoln, NE: University of Nebraska Press, 1986.

Kennedy, Diana. *The Tortilla Book*. New York: Harper & Row, 1975.

Malone, Ann Patton. *Women on the Texas Frontier: A Cross-Cultural Perspective*. Southwestern Studies, Monograph No. 70. El Paso, TX: Texas Western Press, 1983.

McWilliams, Carey. *North From Mexico*. New York: J.B. Lippincott, 1949.

Paredes, Americo. "The Love Tragedy in Texas-Mexican Balladry," *Folk Travelers Ballads, Tales and Talk*. Number XXV, Publication of the Texas Folklore Society. Dallas: Southern Methodist University Press, pp. 110-114, 1928.

Paredes, Americo. *A Texas-Mexican Cancionero: Folksongs of the Lower Border*. Urbana, IL: University of Illinois Press, 1976.

Paredes, Americo. *Folktales of Mexico*. Chicago: University of Chicago Press, 1970.

Paredes, Americo. *With His Pistol in His Hand: A Border Ballad and its Hero*. Austin, TX: University of Texas Press, 1958.

Paz, Octavio. *Sor Juana*. Cambridge, MA: Harvard University Press, 1988.

Poniatowska, Elena. *Guerrero Viejo*. Houston, TX: Anchorage Press, 1997.

Sánchez, José María. "A Trip to Texas in 1828," *The Southwestern Historical Quarterly* (Texas State Historical Association), Vol. XXIX, No. 4 (April 1926): 250-88.

Scott, Florence Johnson. *Historical Heritage of the Lower Río Grande*. San Antonio, TX: Naylor Co., 1937.

Simmons, Marc. *Witchcraft in the Southwest*. Lincoln, NE: University of Nebraska Press, 1980.

Toor, Frances. *Mexican Folkways.* New York: Crown Publishers, 1947.

Webb, Walter Prescott, editor. *The Handbook of Texas.* Austin, TX: Texas State Historical Association, 1952.

About the Author

Trained as a journalist, Laurie Lawlor worked for many years as a freelance writer and editor before devoting herself full-time to the creation of children's books. She enjoys many speaking engagements at schools and libraries, and her books have been nominated for many awards. She lives in Evanston, Illinois, with her husband, son, daughter, and a large Labrador retriever. Her books include the *Addie Across the Prairie* series, the *Heartland* series, *How to Survive Third Grade, The Worm Club, Gold in the Hills,* and *Little Women* (a movie novelization). Her nonfiction work, *Shadow Catcher: The Life and Work of Edward S. Curtis,* won the Carl Sandburg Award for non-fiction (1995) and the Golden Kite Honor Book Award (1995).